[DOUBLE DETECTIVES]

The Secret of Skull Island

by Zack Norris

STERLING CHILDREN'S BOOKS
New York

For Dashiell and Philip

STERLING CHILDREN'S BOOKS
New York

An Imprint of Sterling Publishing
387 Park Avenue South
New York, NY 10016

© 2011 by Dona Smith

ISBN 978-1-4027-7912-1

Library of Congress Cataloging-in-Publication Data
Norris, Zack.
The secret of Skull Island / by Zack Norris.
p. cm. — (Double Detectives ; #1)
Summary: Twins Otis and Cody Carson, their father Hayden, cousin Rae Lee, and family friend Maxim, go to a Caribbean island where Aunt Edith's dream of running an inn is being hampered by ghostly activities and deceitful guests.
ISBN 978-1-4027-7912-1
[1. Swindlers and swindling—Fiction. 2. Taverns (Inns)—Fiction. 3. Islands—Fiction. 4. Brothers—Fiction. 5. Twins—Fiction. 6. Caribbean Area—Fiction. 7. Mystery and detective stories.] I. Title.
PZ7.N7995Sec 2011
[Fic]—dc22

2010046090

Distributed in Canada by Sterling Publishing
⅔ Canadian Manda Group, 165 Dufferin Street
Toronto, Ontario, Canada M6K 3H6
Distributed in the United Kingdom by GMC Distribution Services
Castle Place, 166 High Street, Lewes, East Sussex, England BN7 1XU
Distributed in Australia by Capricorn Link (Australia) Pty. Ltd.
P.O. Box 704, Windsor, NSW 2756, Australia

For information about custom editions, special sales, and premium and corporate purchases, please contact Sterling Special Sales Department at 800-805-5489 or specialsales@sterlingpublishing.com.

Designed by Susan Gerber

Manufactured in the United States of America
Lot #:
2 4 6 8 10 9 7 5 3
10/12

www.sterlingpublishing.com/kids

[Chapter One]

The Boss wasn't happy, and when the Boss wasn't happy, no one in his gang was happy. He was getting angry, too. The gang knew that *that* was a dangerous thing—for all of them. He could take his anger out on anyone.

The gang's head man stood in the shadows, his cell phone pressed tightly to his ear, his guts in a twist. As he listened, his expression went from tense and frightened to angry and resentful. The Boss was chewing him out . . . again.

"I put you in charge of this operation and now I have a mess, Bobo," the Boss snarled. "It's going to mess up our sweet deal. It's going to mess up my money." Bobo heard him exhale through his teeth. "I'm not pleased. What I want is to be pleased."

"Look, Boss, this all happened so fast. How could I have known? It wasn't my fault . . ." the head man protested.

"Stop whining about how it wasn't your fault, Bobo!" the Boss snapped. "You're always supposed to know what's going on."

The Boss breathed into the phone heavily. Bobo could almost see the sneer on the man's face and smell the stink of smoke from his cigar. He hated the way the Boss talked to him and treated him—and the way they all had to call him "Boss."

I'm smarter than any of the other guys in this gang, Bobo thought. *I'm probably smarter than the Boss, too.*

"Bobo, I want you to make this problem go away. I want it fixed, and I want it done *quietly*. Nobody suspects who you are. Nobody knows what's going on. Nobody starts nosing around for *pirate treasure*." He snickered nastily. "And I don't want the law on my back."

"I'm already taking care of it, Boss," blurted Bobo. "I've got the whole plan made up . . ."

"Shut up!" snapped the Boss. "I don't want to hear about your smart ideas, you nitwit. Just do what I told you. And make sure there's no problem with the big job, either."

Bobo heard a click as the Boss ended the conversation without even saying good-bye. He clenched his fists at his sides. He was sick of being ordered around and called names.

"I hate working for this guy," he muttered under his breath. "I ought to have my own outfit. I'd love to give him the double cross."

[Chapter Two]

"The legend says that Calavera Island is haunted by the ghost of a pirate who used the place as his hideout," said twelve-year-old Cody Carson, his brown eyes wide. He turned away from his laptop and glanced at his twin brother, Otis, who looked just like him.

Without looking up from his book, *How to Spot a Liar Every Time*, Otis pushed a lock of brown hair off his forehead, wrinkled his freckled nose, and shrugged. "I don't believe in ghosts," he said. "It's not like it's the first time you've talked—and talked and talked and talked—about that ghost."

Otis reached out and scratched the ears of their golden Labrador named Dude. The dog slapped his tail back and forth in appreciation. The sight caused the parrot, Pauly, to screech in protest. "Pet me! Pet me!" he shrieked.

"Oh, hush, bird," said Rae Lee, the twins' favorite cousin and the coolest girl they knew. Rae was sprawled

4

on the floor next to the boys, a page from the newspaper spread in front of her. Rae's house was nearby, on Cold Stream Lane, and she spent lots of time at her uncle's place.

Deerville, where they all lived, was a small, artsy little town in upstate New York. The twins' father, Hayden Carson, was one of many painters there, and one of the best known. He still lived in the same small farmhouse he'd bought before he was famous, when the twins' mother was still alive. She had died in a car accident when the boys were very young.

"Y'know," Rae said, shaking her short black hair and frowning, "I wouldn't be so sure there aren't any ghosts. There are lots of legends about haunted places. I haven't made up my mind whether they exist or not."

Mr. Carson looked up from his sketchbook. "Well, maybe the pirate's ghost is what has been giving your aunt Edith so much trouble," he said with a chuckle. "I guess we'll find out for ourselves when we get to the island tomorrow."

Aunt Edith was really the boys' great-aunt, their grandmother's sister, but everybody just called her Aunt Edith. She had recently opened an inn on the Caribbean island of Calavera, and there had been trouble from the beginning.

Nearly every day she called long distance about

something that had gone wrong. "It's like this inn is under a black cloud!" she complained.

"What's the latest from Aunt Edith?" Cody asked.

"It sounds like more of the same. Things keep breaking, she runs out of hot water, that sort of thing. Do you think a pirate ghost could be blamed for that?" Mr. Carson asked.

"Ghosts can play all kinds of tricks," Cody said. "Maybe he wants the place to himself again." He turned and looked at everyone solemnly. "A ghost like that could turn ugly and do something really scary."

Rae gave him a sidelong glance. "Too much drama, Cody." She grinned.

Otis groaned. "Way," he agreed. "And way too much talking."

"Oh, I think Aunt Edith's problems are just the kind of things that happen when a new place is opened," said Mr. Carson. "Starting a new business isn't easy." He flipped to a new page in his sketchbook and went on drawing.

"*Calavera* means 'skull' in Spanish, so it's really 'Skull Island,'" Cody went on. "And that pirate I told you about? He had a skull tattooed on his chest. Pirate tattoos had special meanings, you know."

"You've told us that. Lots of times," said Otis. "Blah, blah, blah." He kept his eyes glued to his book.

"*Sit on a potato pan, Otis,*" his brother said cheerfully. Cody loved coming up with palindromes—expressions that are spelled the same backward and forward. "Sit on a potato pan, Otis" was one of his favorites and had been used over and over again.

"You're still using the same old *half-baked* joke," Otis replied with a pun that *he'd* used over and over again. Otis liked puns as much as Cody liked palindromes. And the two brothers loved to kid each other.

"Chill," Cody said, still grinning at his old joke. "Here's something new," he added hurriedly. "The rumor is that the pirate, Black Heart, hid his treasure somewhere on the island. But he forgot where he stashed it, so he comes back to search for it. He also has sword fights with other pirates who are looking for it, too. People swear they have seen and heard him."

His eyes were shining. "Isn't that *great*? Maybe we'll get to meet him while we're on the island. Maybe he'll lead us to the treasure." He frowned. "But the legend says that he'll kill anyone who takes it from him."

"He can't lead you to the treasure if he can't find it himself," Rae pointed out.

Otis laughed. "Yeah, that's kind of obvious."

Cody knitted his brows. "Yeah, I guess you're right." Then his face brightened. "Maybe he'll find it while we're there."

Otis let out a long sigh. "Come on, Cody, grow up. Ghosts? Pirate treasure?"

"You know as well as I do that pirate treasure has been found. They dug up some of Captain Kidd's buried treasure in New York, on Gardiners Island," Cody pointed out. "I'd never even heard of Gardiners Island before I read about Captain Kidd."

"Yeah, I know," said Otis. "But do you *really* still believe in ghosts?"

"Why not?" Cody snapped. "Like Rae said, there are lots of legends about haunted places. And you've seen some of those ghost-hunting shows on TV."

"Those shows are always so lame," Otis scoffed. "Ever notice how they never really find anything? Somehow the ghost never shows up on the videotape."

Mr. Carson held out his sketchbook and studied his drawing. "Well, if there *is* a pirate ghost wandering around, you have a good chance of running into him while we're visiting Aunt Edith," he said. "I was waiting to tell you that your aunt's inn is where the pirate lived years ago. And a hundred or so years before that, the house was part of a sugar plantation. It was the owner's mansion."

"Awesome!" Cody breathed.

"Well, that's pretty interesting," Otis said. "But I still don't believe in ghosts."

From a nearby chair came the sound of a newspaper rustling. "It's nothing but crime, crime, crime in the headlines today," said Maxim Chatterton in a tone that dripped with disdain. He peered from behind the pages and curled his lip.

The worldly and dignified Maxim was the family's all-around friend and helper. He was Mr. Carson's agent, arranging all of his shows and handling his publicity. He was also general overseer of all the household affairs.

"Two bank robberies in downtown Manhattan," Maxim went on, perusing the front page. He shifted his lanky frame. "And here's a story about that Las Vegas gangster Moe Kleese. He got his picture in the paper again. It looks like he's at a party at one of his casinos." He tossed the paper down.

The picture showed a short, round man with a bald head. He had his arms crossed, with one hand showing a huge pinkie ring in the shape of a horseshoe. Around his neck was a showy gold chain with a gold playing card. He was standing underneath the brightly lit sign for one of his casinos—THE LAUGHING GECKO.

"Kleese the sleaze," Maxim muttered, pointing to the picture. "That guy is into everything—theft, smuggling, counterfeiting, you name it. They've never been able to pin anything on him that stuck, though. No wonder he's having a party."

Otis glanced at the paper. "Hey—that's the guy who was on the news last night. I remember him because of the weird way he never made eye contact with the reporter. My book says people who aren't telling the truth don't look you in the eye. They fidget."

"Oh, Otis." Rae crossed her arms. "That book is making you crazy. You're going to start seeing liars everywhere. You get so carried away when something interests you."

"Do not," Otis shot back.

"Um, do *too*," insisted Cody. "A couple of months ago you were into rocks, and that's all you ever talked about. Before that it was insects, and you *bugged* everybody all the time. Now you're going to think every time somebody scratches his nose or shakes his foot, he's lying."

Otis grimaced. "The bugs were Rae's fault. She made that remark, 'Every bug is an insect, but every insect is not a bug,' and I was hooked. I had to find out more. Besides, *you're* pretty fixated on that ghost pirate and his treasure."

"I'm not as bad as you are," Cody retorted. "With you it's always something."

"*Yap, yap, yap.*" Otis laughed.

"Enough, you two," Maxim said sternly. He picked up the paper and rattled it in disgust. "Here's *more* crime. That con artist is still on the loose. Hmm . . . it says he's got a wife somewhere. I wonder if she's a criminal, too. Anyway, he duped some gullible people into buying the Museum of Modern Art. Twice!"

He scanned the article. "Now he's going by a new name—he has about twenty aliases and he's disguised himself as a salesman, a lawyer, a dentist . . . you name it, he's done it. Oh, and listen to this: a thief stole a painting from the museum."

Mr. Carson, who had been sketching quietly, looked up. "It wasn't one of mine, was it?" he asked with a laugh.

"No, no. Van Gogh."

"Terrible." Mr. Carson went back to sketching. "Imagine—Deerville is only a couple of hours from New York City, and it's a different world."

Mr. Carson loved to travel and had painted scenes from Tucson to Tokyo. He was looking forward to taking his family along with him to Calavera Island. It was so small that it was not even on most maps. It was dwarfed by the larger and more developed nearby island of Tacayno.

Just then a command screeched through the air. "Roll over!"

Dude instantly pricked up his ears, dropped, and rolled.

"Ha-ha," scoffed the parrot.

Dude snarled and lay down again, casting an angry eye at Pauly.

Otis went back to his book. Cody went back to researching Calavera Island online, and Rae went back to her paper. Suddenly she gasped.

"A crowd attacked Jamal Mason!" she said, her face pale. "He was making a personal appearance in Hollywood, signing autographs, when the fans got so crazy they rushed at him. Bodyguards got him into a van and drove away."

Fourteen-year-old Jamal Mason was a teen idol, and every kid over four years old followed his movies. He played a brilliant young detective in a series of action-adventure films. The most recent was *The Curse of the Green Dragon*.

Unlike the twins, Rae wasn't a fan of mysteries or action adventure. She preferred drama and comedy—except when it came to Jamal Mason. The twins suspected she had a crush on him, but she always denied it.

"I'll bet Jamal wasn't scared," Cody said. His attention shifted back to Calavera Island.

Rae got to her feet. "I have to be getting home to get ready for the trip," she said. "I'm so glad my parents are letting me come along. See you in the morning."

After everyone said good-bye to Rae, the boys decided to go to bed. They had to get up early for karate class, and then they were all leaving for Calavera Island.

"Why don't you clean up that mess on your side of the room before we go, Cody?" Otis muttered as they headed upstairs.

"I will if you will," Cody replied, giving his brother a little shove. They always argued about which one was messier. Both knew that it was all a joke, though, since they were equally sloppy.

Later on, lying in bed on either side of their messy room, they talked about the trip. Neither one was thrilled that where they were going had no cell phone towers and no Internet access.

"It will be cool to go swimming and explore the island, though," said Otis. "I'm taking my skateboard, too. I'm gonna practice until I get the pop shove-it right. But . . ."

Cody pushed himself up onto his elbows. "You're

going to take your *skateboard*? I like to skateboard, too . . . but we'll be on a Caribbean island. I don't think they'll have a lot of places to skate."

"Maybe you're right," Otis said. Then he put a finger to his lips and whispered, "*Shh*."

Outside their door they could hear their father talking with Maxim. Both of the men were speaking in hushed voices. The boys could just make out what they were saying.

"You know Aunt Edith isn't the type to get scared over nothing," Mr. Carson said.

"I know, I know, but things happen," Maxim replied. "Did she really sound worried?"

"Yes. I didn't want to say so in front of the boys, but she sounded *very* worried. The chandelier in the lobby fell down the other day. Nobody was hurt, but still . . ." Mr. Carson clicked his tongue against his teeth.

"Well, did someone tamper with it?" Maxim asked. "Or was it an accident?"

"She said it *looked* like an accident. But then somebody ruined a bunch of plants in her garden."

"Oh, well, that could have been an animal, right?" Maxim asked.

"I don't think there are any animals on the island that could do that," Mr. Carson replied. "Mostly there are birds and frogs and iguanas and geckos. I can't imagine one of them stampeding through a garden and ripping up plants the way she described. The garden was a wreck."

"But people on the island keep dogs as pets, don't they? It could have been a dog that got loose," Maxim pointed out.

"Oh, you're right. I didn't think of that," Mr. Carson said sheepishly.

The men stopped talking. Their footsteps grew fainter as they walked away.

"Weird," said Cody. "Maybe that falling chandelier wasn't an accident. So many things have gone wrong at the inn . . ."

"You think the pirate ghost is causing trouble?" Otis snorted. "Aunt Edith is just stressed. She's worried about nothing."

He couldn't have been more wrong. At the inn on Calavera Island, there was *plenty* to worry about.

[Chapter Three]

Rae and the twins were still yawning when Maxim dropped them off at the dojo. They were all so excited about the trip to Calavera Island that they had hardly slept. As they took off their shoes, Cody and Otis filled Rae in on what they had overheard.

"Poor Aunt Edith," she said. "It's hard enough just starting a new business, but all those accidents must have her really frazzled." She shook her head.

"Then you don't think it's the pirate's ghost?" Cody asked.

"Not really," she said, while Otis let out an exasperated sigh. Rae smoothed the front of her *gi*. Wearing the karate uniform always made her feel proud. "Anyway, we can't think about it now. We've got to focus on class."

The three of them had learned that the mental part of karate was more important than learning to fight. In fact, the sensei had taught them to avoid a fight whenever possible. But learning to focus and breathe under stress was something they could apply to any situation in life. Now, as junior black belts, they knew it well.

The three waited for the sensei to enter. Soon the master appeared and instructed them to line up. Then he gave the command, "*Mokuso*," meaning, "close your eyes and meditate."

Otis, Cody, and Rae closed their eyes. All thoughts of the upcoming trip and pirate treasure left their minds. The class had begun.

Time passed quickly as they moved through their warm-up exercises. Next, they practiced their stances and then the *katas*—sequences of moves that imitated fighting. Then they paired up to practice techniques of blocking and kicking. Soon they were bowing their good-byes at the closing ceremony.

After class, Maxim and Mr. Carson whisked every-one to the airport. On the plane, Rae and the twins told the two men that they wouldn't be able to relax until they finally got to the island. Then they promptly fell asleep and stayed asleep until the plane landed.

✳

As the Carsons, Maxim, and Rae struggled up the walkway toward the inn through the pouring rain, they didn't know that someone was watching them with binoculars. When Bobo saw Cody, Otis, and Rae he gritted his teeth.

Kids. That's just great, he thought. He tossed the binoculars on the bed and began pacing furiously. *Always gotta poke their runny little noses into everything. Why? They're always asking, "Why, why, why?" It's not enough that I've got to get rid of adults, now I've got to pay attention to kids, too. Who would have thought anyone would bring kids?*

He clenched his fists at his sides. He'd have to be nice to them. They mustn't suspect a thing.

Bobo lifted the binoculars and took another look. "Aw, what's the matter with me?" he muttered, embarrassed. "They're just kids."

He had no idea how much he'd underestimated them.

[Chapter Four]

It was nearly evening before Otis and Cody got their first sight of Calavera Island. They were exhausted and hungry. Their connecting flight had been delayed for hours.

The Carsons, Rae, and Maxim were the only passengers on the tiny plane. Near the end of the flight, the sky had grown dark. As if they came out of nowhere, ominous clouds suddenly filled the sky.

By the time the plane landed, the rain had begun. When the group finally reached the inn, a storm was in full force. The soggy travelers headed up the walk toward the inn.

Wind lashed the palm trees and lightning cracked though the sky, illuminating the ancient mansion with an eerie glow. The huge arched windows seemed to stare out with threatening eyes.

The boys shouldered their bags and trudged up

the walkway, so bedraggled that they didn't bother hurrying through the rain. They exchanged glances. Each knew what the other was thinking. This place sure looked desolate . . . and creepy.

As soon as they reached the front door, it opened with the bone-chilling creak heard in old horror movies. But the boys forgot about their creepy thoughts when they saw the tall woman with waist-length white hair and sparkling eyes.

"What's up, Aunt Edith?" they asked together.

"We'll talk about it later," their aunt said hurriedly. "You all have to get up to your rooms and get dried off. Then come on down to dinner. You must be starving."

She showed the group to their rooms. The boys couldn't help noticing that their aunt seemed anxious and distracted. It was a change from her usual cheerful enthusiasm. In fact, they had never seen her act that way.

*

Half an hour later they were seated around the dining room table with the other guests, who had arrived days earlier. There weren't many—only six of them—two women and four men, all about the same age as Mr. Carson.

"Everybody, please join me in welcoming our new guests—my family. This is Hayden Carson, my nephew; his sons, Cody and Otis; and their cousin Rae Lee. Hayden's sister married Rae's father while she was visiting Hong Kong," she said pleasantly. "Rae was born two years later. It's such a romantic story."

"I think that's enough information, Aunt Edith," Rae said, rolling her eyes.

Aunt Edith chuckled. "They've brought along their good friend Maxim Chatterton. Would all of you please introduce yourselves and add a bit of information?" She gave everyone a big smile, but it didn't match her eyes. Cody and Otis thought her cheerfulness seemed forced. What was wrong with Aunt Edith?

"Before we start, I have something to tell you," Aunt Edith said. The smile on her face tightened. "Our wonderful cook was called away on family business."

"Just like the guide? Why is all the help leaving the place?" asked one of the guests, a man of about thirty-five with blond hair and blue eyes and a heavy, fake-looking tan. The twins didn't like his tone. There was something nasty about it.

Aunt Edith just shrugged. "Until I find someone else, I'll be preparing the meals. Tonight we have a lovely cream of mushroom soup and a casserole. I hope you'll enjoy the meal."

Aunt Edith nodded to a young woman with dark hair and eyes who had been standing quietly near the kitchen doorway. "Go ahead and begin serving the soup, Inez," she said. "Now, let's all introduce ourselves."

"I'm Cody Carson," Cody blurted eagerly. "And I—"

"Hold on, Cody," Mr. Carson cut in. "Never the shy one," he said with a chuckle. "I'd like to hear from the folks who've been staying here on the island first."

Aunt Edith turned to the man with the fake tan. "All right, then. Why don't you start, Mr. Cordell?"

"Why, sure." The man cleared his throat. He looked up at the ceiling as he spoke. Then he pushed his water glass out in front of his plate.

"I'm Steve Cordell, and I'm a real-estate broker from California. The business is always go, go, go, so I came here to take it easy. That's about it."

"What's the price per square foot for an apartment out there?" asked Otis, his eyes boring into the man.

Cody gulped. Since when was Otis interested in real estate? Suddenly he realized what Otis was up to. He was trying to find out if the man was lying.

"Um—well, I'm surprised you're interested," Mr.

Cordell said. "We can't price apartments like linoleum tile. Knowing how much an apartment is worth comes with experience," he said quickly.

Maxim stared at Otis, his mouth set in a thin line. He also realized what Otis was up to. He shook his head slowly. Otis got the message: no more questions.

The gray-haired man next to Steve Cordell scratched his chin. "I'm Eric Barber from Indiana," he said. He pulled his ear and shifted in his chair. "I own a shoe store."

For some reason the woman next to Mr. Barber glared at him before she introduced herself. "I'm Helen Wallace from Virginia," she said, twirling a piece of her brown bob. She looked down at her plate and shrugged. "I'm a retired librarian, and I love to ski."

When Ms. Wallace was silent for a moment, the woman next to her spoke up. "I'm Muriel Esposito," she said, "and I own a little sewing shop in Maryland." Her brown ponytail swished as she turned to Mr. Carson and smiled. "I'm a great fan of your work. I just love your paintings!"

"Agreed!" said the man on her right enthusiastically. His name was Sam Keller, and he was pale with red hair and green eyes. Keller couldn't stop tapping his foot as he told them that he worked in a post office in New Jersey.

Lastly, a man with thinning dark hair and brown eyes introduced himself as Albert McNab. "I own a little corner grocery store in Brooklyn, New York," he said with a grin that lit up his face like sunshine. "It's the first chance I've had to get away in years. Mr. Carson, I've admired your paintings, too."

Steve Cordell's eyes narrowed. "I've been wondering how a small-time grocery owner has the money to buy himself a Rolex watch," he said, staring at the gold timepiece on McNab's wrist.

It was such a rude comment that everyone was shocked. But no one knew what to say.

McNab didn't look as if he were offended in the least. "Oh, I suppose that's a reasonable thing to wonder," he said with a smile at Cordell. "I've been very lucky with my investments in the stock market. Anyone can do the same, really. I'd be happy to help you start an investment portfolio, if you like."

"Nah, I don't need any help," muttered Cordell.

By now Inez, the maid, had served everyone bowls of cream of mushroom soup. Cody looked down at his and bit his lip. He had never seen soup look so much like dishwater. He dipped his spoon and swallowed.

Ugh! It took every bit of willpower that he had to stop from spitting it out. He looked at Otis and saw that his nose was wrinkled. Then he gazed around the table and saw that he wasn't the only one who didn't like the food.

Maxim's mouth was puckered as if he'd just bitten into a lemon. His face was beet red. Almost everyone else was grimacing, too.

Only Aunt Edith and Mr. Carson seemed not to notice anything wrong. Both swallowed spoonful after spoonful of soup.

The casserole was even worse. The guests pushed around their portions on their plates.

The twins, Rae, Maxim, and Mr. Carson introduced themselves. Then Cody asked if anyone thought the place was haunted. That got everybody talking.

"*I* definitely think so," Muriel Esposito said, leaning forward. "I've heard footsteps in the hallway sometimes, but no one is there!"

McNab nodded. "I believe it, too," he said. "The other day I was walking in the garden, and all of a sudden footprints started appearing on the path just like somebody was walking beside me." He paused and looked around the table. "But there wasn't anybody there. Nobody I could see, anyway."

"Oh, this place is haunted, all right," Barber agreed. "I've heard those footsteps in the hallway, just as Ms. Esposito has."

"Me, too," said Ms. Wallace. She lifted up a forkful

of casserole and examined it before returning it to her plate.

"I heard the pirate talking," said Steve Cordell. He rubbed his nose. "He was telling me to leave his treasure alone. He sounded pretty threatening. Maybe he's the one who made the chandelier fall down."

"How could a ghost make a chandelier fall down?" Otis asked, looking darkly at Cordell. It seemed as if he wanted people to be scared.

"Well, I think it's all pretty frightening," Sam Keller said in a hushed tone. He tapped his foot nervously. "I know it scares *me*."

When nobody said anything, the man threw up his hands. "Well? Come on now, isn't anybody else scared?"

McNab started to chuckle. His laughter was so contagious that most of the other guests joined in. "Y'know, I think it's just a whole lot of fun. I always wanted to go to a haunted house. When I called up to book the place and Edith told me it might be haunted, I thought she was pulling my leg, but doggone it, the place is haunted all right. Hot dog!"

Nearly everybody seemed to agree with him. They weren't scared. In fact, they *wanted* to be in a place that was haunted. It was cool.

"Maybe the ghost is the reason that the cook and the guide left," Cordell said slowly. "Things have been going wrong here from the beginning. We didn't have hot water for two days. Maybe that's the ghost, too. It's going to be hard to keep a staff."

"Well, I don't think so," said McNab. He threw his napkin down beside his plate. "We heard the cook and the guide left because of family business, and I believe what I was told. If I'm not scared of the ghost, why would they be?" He glared at Cordell. "It sounds to me like you're trying to spoil the fun, and I, for one, don't appreciate it."

An uncomfortable silence fell over the table. The twins were surprised that McNab had gotten angry. He was such a pleasant man. But they agreed with him about Cordell. He seemed determined to spoil the fun.

"Oh, forget what I said," McNab told everyone after a moment. "I guess I'm just tired." He smiled his sunny smile once more.

"Hardly anyone touched their food," said Aunt Edith, her brow puckered with disappointment.

"I think we're all just too tired to eat," replied Maxim. He was always a gentleman.

The other guests hurriedly agreed. They yawned

loudly and insisted that they were all exhausted. One by one they headed to their rooms, including Mr. Carson.

"Well, I'm afraid I'm exhausted, too," Aunt Edith said. "I'll chat with you all tomorrow. Good night." She plucked nervously at her sundress as she walked away.

Finally, only Maxim, Rae, and the twins were left sitting at the table. Maxim let out a groan as soon as Aunt Edith was out of earshot.

"What a dreadful, dreadful meal," he cried. "Cream of mushroom soup, indeed! It was more like cream of *washroom*. And that casserole! A combination of chili squares and cheese chow mein."

The boys both doubled over, but Maxim cut their laughter short. He pointed a finger at Otis. "You're obsessed with that book of yours. Don't start cross-examining people again. You'll be finding liars everywhere! Good night, kids."

"Well, I think there *are* plenty of liars here," Otis said after Maxim was gone. "What a twitchy bunch! Did you see how that tan guy, Cordell, never made eye contact? Sure sign of a liar. And the way he put his water glass in front of him? The book says that liars put objects between themselves and others, as if they want to hide behind something."

Cody nodded. "Everybody *was* tapping and scratching and moving around. Except for Mr. McNab and Ms. Esposito. But I'm not sure that it means all the others were lying."

Otis tilted his head to one side. "I wonder if *family business* was the real reason the cook left. I have a feeling something is going on here, don't you?"

Cody shrugged. "Maybe. The place has a weird vibe, all right."

"Oh, come on now," said Rae. "We're on an island paradise and all you guys can think about is some kind of mystery. First it was buried treasure, and now it's *something weird going on*."

As soon as the words were out of her mouth, a bloodcurdling shriek ripped through the air. Rae and the boys jumped up from the table and raced upstairs.

They found all the guests gathered in the hallway, clad in pajamas. They were gawking at Aunt Edith, who was screaming at the top of her lungs.

"It's a cobra! Or a python! Or a copperhead!" she cried. "Right on my bed!"

Everyone seemed frozen in shock. Cody and Otis tiptoed into her room. There, curled up on the blue cotton bedspread, was an orange and gold snake at least six feet long.

[Chapter Five]

It certainly looked like a deadly snake. It raised its head and looked at the boys.

Otis looked the snake in the eyes. "This is no venomous snake," he said firmly. "Cody, give me a hand."

Otis moved quickly and grabbed the snake behind the head. Then Cody grabbed the tail.

As everyone stared, the boys hurried downstairs and outside with the snake. They walked a distance from the inn and set it free behind some trees. They both watched it slither away.

"Well, that's that," Otis said, wiping his hands on his shorts. "I wonder where that thing came from."

Cody shrugged. "We'd better get back and explain why we grabbed it," he said. "Everybody will be freaking out."

They were right. When they got back to the inn, everyone was downstairs waiting for them. Aunt Edith was sitting at the dining room table, shaking.

"What on earth were you boys thinking, grabbing that snake?" she asked, her voice quivering. All of the color had drained from her face.

"Yes, what in the world were you doing?" snapped their father.

"That was a dangerous stunt," said Maxim.

Otis held up a hand for silence. "But the snake wasn't venomous, so it wasn't dangerous," he said. "In fact, people keep snakes like that for pets. It was a corn snake. I know, because of helping out in the pet store, Pets Plus, for years. They sell corn snakes there. I've handled them many times, and I know one when I see one."

"Yeah, I didn't realize it at first," said Cody. "Otis is more into snakes than I am. As soon as he said it wasn't venomous I knew it was a corn snake, though. They look a lot like copperheads, but they're gentle."

"How could you be *sure* that it wasn't dangerous?" asked Albert McNab.

"Like I said, I've handled them lots of times. But besides that, there is an interesting fact about snakes," Otis said. "You see, non-venomous snakes like this one have round pupils. Snakes with venom in their fangs have vertical pupils, like a cat does."

Otis glanced at Rae. "She's the one who told me about it," he said with a nod.

The guests blinked as they looked at Rae. "That's right," she said. "I read about it in a textbook of ophiology that my brother brought home from college." She shrugged.

"But the study of snakes is *herpetology,* dear," corrected Ms. Wallace.

"Um, actually, no, ma'am," Rae said, looking at her own shoes. "Herpetology is the study of snakes and other reptiles. Ophiology is the study of only snakes."

Ms. Wallace fluttered her lashes and raised a hand to her cheek. "Well, well, now that I think of it, you're quite right."

The guests murmured in surprise. All peered at the boys and the girl, their eyes moving from one to the other. "Almost like they're kids—but *not really,*" whispered McNab under his breath. "They're like walking computers."

"I have very, very, very good eyesight," Otis went on. "I looked at the snake's eyes carefully. I wouldn't recommend anyone doing what Cody and I did unless you are one hundred percent sure of the kind of snake you are dealing with. It could be deadly."

"Oh, goodness, I don't like the idea of snakes crawling into my bed," said Muriel Esposito. Her body shivered as she spoke.

"Well, it's an island, after all," said Steve Cordell. "Islands have snakes. It could happen again, you know." He ignored the glare he got from McNab.

"The trouble is," said Otis, "that this island shouldn't have this snake. Corn snakes aren't native to the Caribbean. They live in the southeastern United States. Someone must have brought it here."

"Anyone lost a pet corn snake?" asked Cody.

The guests were silent. Finally Cordell's face lit up with a grin. "I think that maybe it belongs to one of you kids." He chuckled. "You knew it wasn't dangerous. Kids like to play pranks. Maybe you decided to have a little fun with your aunt."

"My sons didn't bring any snakes with them," snapped Mr. Carson.

"It isn't even an amusing suggestion," Maxim added, as Rae gave Cordell an icy glare.

"And if anyone played such a silly prank, it certainly wasn't my nephews," Aunt Edith said indignantly.

Cordell held up his hands and backed away, but he was still grinning. "Whoa! I was just kidding around."

Otis scowled at him. "Not funny," said Cody.

Everyone began heading back to their rooms. As the boys passed by they saw Inez, the maid, standing there lost in thought, a strange expression on her face.

Back in their room, Cody leaned against the door. "I didn't like what that guy Cordell said," he fumed.

"Me neither," Otis agreed. "I didn't like the way he was acting before, either. There is something else about him that bothers me, too." He yawned. "But I'm too tired to think anymore."

"Me, too," Cody agreed. In moments they were fast asleep.

✴

When Cody woke up, the light of the moon was streaming through the window. His brother was already sitting up in bed. "I heard something," he said.

Cody rubbed his eyes. "What?" Then he heard it, too. *Thud, thud, thud, thud.* "It sounds like footsteps coming from the hallway. Do you think it's the pirate?"

"I don't know," Otis whispered. He had to admit that at that moment his certainty about ghosts had gone right out the window.

The two boys slipped out of bed and opened the door slowly. "Who's there?" rasped a voice. They knew it wasn't one of the guests.

"Who's there?" the voice asked again. *Thud, thud, thud, thud.* The footsteps came closer.

Neither Cody nor Otis was able to move. Their

legs felt like jelly. They both stood still as the footsteps thudded closer.

"I'm looking for my treasure," the voice whispered. "*Ahhhhhh . . .*"

The sound faded away. The twins waited, their hearts beating fast, but there were no more footsteps. After several minutes they turned and walked slowly back to bed. Neither one dared to say a word.

[Chapter Six]

The next morning was sunny and clear. A gentle breeze was blowing. As the twins looked out their window, they saw the landscape was a riot of color. There were green trees and rainbows of flowers as far as the eye could see. Colorful birds flew through the air. The creepy feeling the place had held the night before had vanished.

"Did we really hear that ghost last night?" Cody asked Otis.

Otis nodded slowly. "I think so, but I'm just not sure I wasn't dreaming. All that talk about it at the table might have played a trick on my mind. Maybe you were dreaming, too."

Cody considered what he said. Sometimes he and his brother had the same dream—it was the kind of thing that sometimes happened to twins. "Maybe," he said.

There was a rapping on the door. "Come on, you guys, get going." It was Rae's voice.

The twins hurried to get dressed, then they ran downstairs with Rae.

In the dining room they found Maxim wearing a kitchen apron. He had laid out a buffet of fresh fruit and muffins, coffee, tea, and juice.

He smiled when he saw them. "This is more like it," he said, gesturing at the buffet. "People can eat like they're on a Caribbean island instead of stranded in a bad cafeteria."

He motioned Rae and the twins aside. "I had a talk with your aunt Edith. I'll be in charge of the kitchen until she can hire someone," he said. "Meanwhile, I don't want you talking to her about what happened last night. She's upset enough as it is."

The three of them nodded. "Where's Dad?" asked Cody.

"He ate early, packed up his gear, and went out to paint," Maxim told them. "He took a sleeping bag with him and said he might stay out overnight—or *nights*. You know how he is."

Rae and the twins were used to Mr. Carson's ways. Sometimes he would spend days doing nothing but painting, barely stopping to eat or sleep.

Aunt Edith breezed in from the kitchen. She didn't look like the same person who had been scared out of her wits the night before.

"You youngsters should go down to the beach," she said. "It looks like a spectacular day for swimming and snorkeling. There is a big chest with some gear right out back."

"Sounds like a plan." Rae grinned. She loved to swim.

"Sure does," Cody and Otis agreed. They exchanged glances. The night before, Cody had convinced Otis to help him look for the buried treasure.

"Hey, Rae," Cody asked as they were putting together plates of fresh fruit and glasses of juice, "did you hear any weird noises last night?"

"No way," she said, helping herself to a muffin. "I was practically asleep before my head hit the pillow."

They took a seat at the table, where most of the guests were drinking coffee. Steve Cordell was telling everyone how he maintained his great tan.

"I never let it fade. It's as perfect as it is now twenty-four-seven, three hundred and sixty-five days of the year. Want to know my secret? When I travel for work, if it isn't sunny out, I go to a tanning parlor. Plus, I have my own tanning bed."

The twins both stifled a giggle. It struck them as funny that this man would be so obsessed with tanning that he bought a tanning bed. They wondered, too, why a California real-estate broker needed to travel for work.

Everyone else looked bored—except for Albert McNab, who kept nodding as if he were hanging on Cordell's every word. "My goodness, that's very interesting," he said.

Cody took a sip of juice and asked, "Anyone hear the ghost last night?"

"I did," said Ms. Wallace. Her eyes danced. "It was incredible. He walked right down the hallway and talked about his treasure. It was wonderful."

"What's so wonderful about being woken up in the middle of the night by a ghost?" Cordell asked. "At least we had hot water this morning."

Eric Barber took a seat. He shot a sour look at Cordell. "I couldn't help overhearing," he said. "You seem to be spreading good cheer again this morning."

Nobody said anything. The twins munched on their food. Cody was going to mention that he and Otis had also heard the ghost, when suddenly a cry of pain shattered the silence.

Everyone rushed to see what it was and found

Muriel Esposito with one foot all the way through a porch step. She was holding her knee and rocking back and forth.

"I think it's broken," she sobbed. "I think my leg is broken."

McNab hurried to her. "Can you pull your leg out?" he asked gently. "Let's have a look at it."

Trembling, Ms. Esposito drew her leg through the broken wood. As soon as the leg was free, McNab gasped. "Oh, no! Look over there, in the bushes," he exclaimed.

Everyone looked around, and when they looked back, McNab's hand was clasped around Ms. Esposito's leg below the knee. "It's not broken," he said firmly.

She looked down, astonished. "What—"

"You were just surprised and frightened," McNab said gently, withdrawing his hand. "That bone is strong. If it had been broken you would have screamed as soon as I grabbed it. Trust me. You have a little scratch, that's all. You'll be fine."

"Thank goodness for that," said Maxim. "Come on back in and have a cup of coffee, Muriel, and some fresh-squeezed pineapple juice. I picked the pineapples this morning and the juice is delicious. It'll fix you right up." He beamed.

Ms. Esposito smiled weakly. "Thank you," she whispered. She turned to Mr. McNab. "Thank you so much."

"I'm just glad you're all right," McNab said, giving her a warm smile. He threw an arm around her shoulders and walked her back inside.

Strangely, the other guests weren't smiling. Cody and Otis were puzzled by their reactions.

Helen Wallace and Eric Barber were exchanging meaningful looks. But why?

Steve Cordell was looking at Sam Keller with an angry expression. Keller seemed annoyed. He kept huffing and pacing back and forth.

Aunt Edith seemed nervous, too. Of course, she *would* be upset at having one more accident happen. Inez looked even more nervous than Aunt Edith.

The twins and Rae stayed behind when the others went inside. They all examined the broken step. After a moment, the twins looked at each other and nodded. They had both recognized the same thing.

The wood grain on the broken step didn't match the grain on the other steps. In fact, it looked like a different kind of wood entirely. And the nails were brand-new and shiny, not dull like the others.

"Somebody planned this," said Cody. "They just

pried up the step and replaced the board with another that was thin in the middle. I wonder who changed it—and when."

"They had plenty of time to sneak down here when everyone else was asleep," said Otis. "They probably had the step loosened already—then they just had to pry it up and replace it with the board they had prepared. The nails probably slipped into the worn holes easily, with mostly pushing and hardly any pounding," he said. "After all, they weren't building something that was supposed to last. It had another purpose."

"Yeah, it sure did. Do you think whoever it was wanted to hurt Ms. Esposito?" Cody asked.

"Nah," Otis replied. "I think they just wanted *somebody* to get hurt."

"The question is . . . why?"

"Oh—you two mystery freaks," Rae said, hands on her hips. "Maybe the step was repaired with a piece of wood that didn't match. So what? The accident could have been just that—an accident."

The boys had to admit that she could be right. But they couldn't help thinking that maybe, just maybe, they had stumbled into a mystery.

When the three went back inside, Helen Wallace and Eric Barber were seated across from Ms. Esposito and Mr. McNab.

"You handled that situation so professionally," Ms. Wallace told him. "You distracted Muriel so quickly and took her mind off what happened to her leg. It was like you had experience with such things."

"Yes, indeed," Mr. Barber agreed. "And you were so sure the way you grabbed her leg to see if it was broken." He gave out a little chuckle. "If you hadn't told me otherwise, I'd think you were a doctor."

"Oh, that's quite a stretch." Mr. McNab laughed. "I've been a scoutmaster for many years. You have to learn about first aid to take a group of scouts into the wilderness. I just acted on instinct. Fortunately, it worked out."

"Oh, come now. Are you sure you haven't had any medical training?" Ms. Wallace persisted.

Mr. McNab blinked. "No, it's just as I told you. I am a scoutmaster, and I know first aid. Beyond that, I just know it's important to try to get someone who is injured to calm down."

The twins watched Ms. Wallace and Mr. Barber give each other meaningful looks again. It was clear that they suspected something about McNab. But what?

"Has anyone else here ever been a scoutmaster?" McNab asked. "It's very rewarding. How about you, Cordell—ever led a scouting troop?"

Steve Cordell acted as if he hadn't heard a word. He sat there staring into space, drumming his fingers on the table. When McNab repeated the question, he looked at him and blinked and then mumbled, "Aw, what a waste of time."

Sam Keller threw down his napkin abruptly. He glanced at Cordell and muttered, "I think I'll take a walk. See ya later, Jimmy."

Cordell slapped his hand on the table loudly enough to make everyone stop talking. He stood up and called to Keller, "Don't call me Jimmy," he snapped. "My name is Steve, remember?"

Keller did a double take and turned around. "I'm s-sorry, S-Steve," he stammered. "I didn't mean to, uh, offend you."

Cordell was fuming. But after a moment he blushed scarlet and sat down again. He looked around the table. "Sorry, everyone, I'm kind of edgy. I didn't get enough sleep. That ghost woke me up."

There were shrugs and murmurs as everyone assured Cordell that he was forgiven. Cody and Otis were thinking the same thing—that this guy was really wound up. And they were surer than ever that he was hiding something.

Meanwhile, Rae announced that she was going off

for a swim. "I can't wait to get in that water," she told the twins as she hurried away.

Later, when breakfast was over and the other guests were heading their separate ways, Otis turned to Cody and whispered, "Did you see how angry Steve Cordell got when Keller called him Jimmy by mistake?"

"Yeah—it was really weird."

"I've figured out what it is about him that bothers me," said Otis. "It's that I know I've seen him somewhere before. I feel like I should know who he is, but I just can't think why." He frowned and shook his head.

"I know we planned to hunt for the buried treasure, but first let's follow Cordell and see where he goes," said Cody. "I just have one of those hunches I get sometimes. We might learn something."

Both boys had gotten those "hunches" from time to time. They had learned to trust them.

"Let's do it," Otis agreed. "I'm pretty sure that he headed out to the garden. What about Rae, though? We should tell her what we're doing."

"Rae will be happy swimming," said Cody. "We'll catch up with her later. She won't want to spy on Cordell, and she wouldn't want to hunt for buried treasure, either. Not with that beautiful ocean out there. Let's go."

The boys found Steve Cordell and Sam Keller seated on a bench not far from the inn. The two were having a heated discussion. Cordell was flailing his arms around as he spoke. Keller was pointing and punching the air.

The twins made every movement as quiet as a whisper. They crept closer and closer to the two men, who were caught up in their argument.

"You're an idiot," Cordell said, his face thrust close to Keller's. "You're just a stupid, careless idiot. Why did you call me Jimmy?"

Keller pounded his fist on the arm of the bench. "Now you hold on just a minute, Jimmy," he began.

"Stop calling me Jimmy!" Cordell exploded. "Do you want people to know who we are? We're supposed to keep it a secret. You'll ruin everything."

"Okay, okay . . . *Steve*," Keller said with a sneer in his voice. "If anybody will blow our cover, it'll be you. Why did you have to make such a big deal out of a little slip? People who've just met do it all the time."

It made sense. But Cordell just blustered on.

"People do it all the time? Well, you're not supposed to do it. I had a plan all worked out. All we have to do is follow it."

Keller snorted. "Well, excuse me if I say that your

plan doesn't seem to be working too well. Look at what just happened. I think—"

"Don't think," Cordell cut him off. "Just do what I told you. And don't screw up anymore."

"I've had just about enough of you bossing me around," said Keller, pointing a finger at Cordell. "Who do you think you are? And don't you ever, *ever* call me an idiot again."

Cordell opened his mouth to say something. But at that very moment Otis stepped on a twig. It snapped with a loud *crack*!

The twins froze as both men jumped. "What was that?" said Cordell. "Who's there?"

The twins' hearts hammered in their chests. Each one held his breath as he backed up silently and quickly. Then they turned and ran. They didn't stop running until they got to the garden.

[Chapter Seven]

Their chests were heaving by the time the twins got to the garden. They stopped and leaned against some rocks to catch their breath.

"I don't think they knew it was us back there. It's a miracle they didn't run after us," said Cody.

"We were pretty quiet."

"So why do you think that Cordell and Keller are hiding who they are?"

Otis shrugged. "I don't know, but I think it's got something to do with whatever it is I can't remember about Cordell."

"We should tell Dad and Maxim," Cody said.

"I know," Otis agreed. "But we can't prove they are doing anything wrong. Maxim and Dad will think that I'm just getting carried away because of the book about liars I've been reading."

Cody nodded. "That's what I thought, too. Now I

think they need some detectives around here. But Dad and Maxim probably wouldn't agree."

"Keller and Cordell would deny everything. They'd say we misunderstood what they said, or didn't hear it right," said Otis.

"I don't like keeping secrets from Dad," said Cody.

"Neither do I," said Otis. "But all we know now is that those guys are hiding who they really are. It's not like we heard them planning to rob a bank. Let's get something we can prove."

They heard a rustling noise and looked up to find a wiry old gentleman in a broad straw hat. There were pruning shears in his hand.

"Afternoon, boys, I'm the gardener. Winston Cato's the name." He smiled. His voice was soft, lilting—a mix of accents. "Do you remember that I picked you up at the airport? It was raining pretty hard that night."

"I recognize your voice," said Otis.

"Me, too," Cody said. "We were keeping our heads down because of the rain."

"Yes, it was real bad. You Carson twins are getting famous around here. Everybody's talking about how you and your cousin saved Aunt Edith from the snake."

"You heard about the snake already?" Otis asked.

"Oh, sure," Cato chuckled. "I hear most things right away."

"Have you been on the island a long time?" Cody asked eagerly.

"Born here," Cato answered, bending to examine a rose bush.

"Then have you heard about the pirate and the lost buried treasure?"

Cato stood up and nodded. "Sure have . . . but I couldn't tell you how to go about finding it. Nobody ever laid hands on a map . . . least as far as I know."

Cody sighed. Otis shrugged. "Without a map we're kind of up a creek without a paddle," he said.

"Do you have some shovels you could lend us, Mr. Cato?" Cody asked.

"You don't give up easily, do you?" Cato said with a grin. He walked to a shed and returned with two shovels.

"Thanks," Cody said, taking them and handing one to Otis.

"Now we just need to know where to dig."

"Right," Cody agreed. "I've got an idea. C'mon."

The twins said good-bye to Winston Cato, who wished them good luck. As they walked, Cody told Otis his idea.

"I've heard stories about people tattooing maps on their bodies," he said. "Maybe the pirate's skull tattoo is a marker."

"So all we've got to do is look all over the island for the skull, right?"

"Yeah." Cody nodded enthusiastically.

"Ever wonder why the pirate can't find the treasure when he had the marker tattooed on his own chest?" Otis asked, and faced Cody with his arms crossed.

"Well—I dunno," Cody replied.

A couple of hours later they found the answer to the question. They found a skull marker, all right. It was scratched into a rock. But then they dug and dug and dug under the rock and found nothing.

They found two more skull markers and dug under them. They had the same result as before. Zip. Nada. Nothing.

"No wonder that pirate can't find his treasure. There are markers all over the place," said Otis. He leaned on the handle of his shovel and mopped his sweaty brow.

"I guess he left fake markers everywhere to out-smart others who were trying to look for the treasure," said Cody, taking a seat on a rock. He wiped his dirty hands on his shorts.

"Well, he ended up outsmarting himself, didn't he?" Otis raised his eyebrows. Both boys burst out laughing.

Cody slapped his knee with his hand. "I think I've had it. For today, anyway. Let's go down to the beach and find Rae. I could use a swim."

They found Rae sliding on the waves on her boogie board. She waved when she saw them. "Where have you guys been?"

They told her about the treasure hunt. Then they filled her in on what they had heard Cordell and Keller talking about. "I still think there is some treasure on the island," Cody said.

"Maybe—or maybe it's just a hoax," said Rae. "As for your mystery, I can't get excited about it. Why worry about a couple of grumpy guys when there is this beautiful island with this perfect blue water? Look at it!" She ran and plunged into the waves.

The twins looked out at the great ocean. Seabirds dotted the sky and swooped down over the water.

Cody squished sand between his toes. He smelled the scent of the sea and the flowers and trees. He forgot about Cordell and Keller and the mystery.

Otis dipped his toes into the water. "It looks like your treasure marker idea was *all wet*," he said.

"I haven't given up yet." Cody gave him a lopsided smile. "Come on, let's go for a swim."

The two boys plunged into the surf. The water was crystal clear and cool. Colorful fish swam all around them.

The twins swam for over an hour. Then they left Rae, who insisted on staying in the surf, and walked slowly back to the inn. They left the shovels in the garden shed and then headed up the walkway, past some iguanas and geckos standing on rocks that lined the path. The reptiles were so still they looked like green spiky-headed statues.

The step had been fixed. The new board looked strong and sturdy.

"That was fast," Cody observed.

The twins entered the kitchen, where they found Aunt Edith and Maxim sitting at the table in the dining room. The adults looked up as the boys walked in.

"We've just been talking about cooking," said Aunt Edith. "I had no idea Maxim used to be a chef."

"He's done a *lot* of things," Cody said. "Hey, Aunt Edith, you got that step fixed pretty fast."

"Yes. Shortly after the accident, Mr. Cordell came to me and insisted on fixing the step so that no one else would get hurt. He even apologized for getting so angry—isn't that nice?"

"Oh," Otis said softly.

"Is something wrong?"

"No—no. We were just wondering how it broke the way it did. It held us all when we were entering. And then we noticed that the wood on the step that broke didn't look the same as on the other boards."

Aunt Edith put her hands on her hips. "But they were all replaced at the same time. That would be very odd."

"Yes, wouldn't it?" Cody nodded. "But think about it. Why did it break all of a sudden?"

Maxim was shaking his head. "I see that you are determined to be detectives. There is a perfectly reasonable explanation. Apparently an animal has been scratching and gnawing away at it. Finally the step was so weak that poor Ms. Esposito went through it."

The boys exchanged glances. Just as they thought, Maxim was sure the boys were only getting carried away with the game of being detectives.

"What happened to the broken board?" asked Otis. "Do you know where it is?"

"I imagine that Mr. Cordell tossed it on the rubbish heap behind the house," said Aunt Edith. "But I don't think you'd find it. There is a mountain of stuff left back there from the renovation that I've got to get carted away." She thumbed over her shoulder.

Otis and Cody walked to the window and stared

out at an immense mountain of tangled lumber and plaster. It was very unlikely that they'd locate the board there.

As they walked from the kitchen they talked about what they'd been told. It just didn't seem right that it all fit together so neatly and innocently.

"Well, we didn't exactly *nail* that one," Otis remarked.

"No, we didn't." Cody sighed. He paused for a moment, listening. "Do you hear water running?"

Otis tilted his head. "Yes, I do. It sounds like a *lot* of water."

The boys hurried in the direction of the sound. It was coming from the bathroom in the lobby, gurgling and whooshing.

By the time they reached the bathroom, water was rushing out from underneath the door. They opened it and saw water all over the floor, pouring from the toilet tank.

Maxim and Aunt Edith ran up behind them. "Oh, no!" cried their aunt as she looked at the flood.

Cody bent down and turned the knob that shut off the water. Otis grabbed some towels off the rack and threw them down to soak up the water. Then he took the top off the tank and peered inside.

"This is a nightmare!" Aunt Edith wailed. "I think a pipe burst!"

Rae appeared, her towel slung around her neck. She eyed the overflowing toilet. "No, no, Aunt E.— it's not that bad," she said. "I think the toilet just overflowed. The water kept running because the overflow tube was clogged up."

"What's that?" asked Aunt Edith.

"It's a tube where water drains from the tank back into the bowl. The flotation device has been tampered with, too. There was no way for the tank to 'know' that it was full. So the water just kept on running."

"Did you read that in a plumbing textbook?" Maxim asked. "Honestly, Rae, the things you and the twins know never cease to amaze me." He chuckled.

"We had that problem when a contractor redid our bathroom, that's all," said Rae.

"We'll just clean it out then, right, Cody?" Otis said. Cody nodded. "Don't worry, Aunt Edith."

"I'm going to run and change," said Rae. "See you all later." She took off up the stairs. On her way, she passed Albert McNab.

Aunt Edith raised a hand to her forehead. "It's one thing after another since I've opened this place. I'm just worn out."

"Now, now, calm down, dear," Maxim said gently.

"I can't calm down," said Aunt Edith. "This wasn't an accident."

Cody shook his head. "Can you think of anyone who would want to sabotage the inn?"

Aunt Edith sucked in her breath. She hesitated a moment and then said, "Actually, there might be someone who would. I had to fire a worker. He was always late, left early, disappeared for hours. He was pretty angry when I let him go."

"Maybe he came sneaking back here and made sure some things went wrong," said Cody.

Aunt Edith looked thoughtful. "Do you mean that maybe he drained the hot water heater and caused the chandelier to fall and put that snake in my bed?"

"It's possible," Cody replied. He rinsed the dirt and pebbles from the return tube and fixed the flotation device. "Good as new," he announced.

"I hope we'll get to relax for a while." Aunt Edith sighed.

"Well, I'm not feeling very relaxed," said a voice in the doorway. They looked up and saw McNab. "My room has been ransacked," he said.

[Chapter Eight]

The room had been ransacked, all right. The mattress had been pulled off the bed, the linens and pillows scattered everywhere. The clothes had been pulled off the hangers in the closet and were piled on the floor. Every drawer had been dumped out.

"Look at that note," McNab said, pointing to a piece of paper taped to the inside of his door. Written in jagged letters that looked almost as if they'd been slashed into the paper were the words, *Get out while you can.*

"What a mess! What happened?" said a woman's voice outside the door. It was Muriel Esposito, and when she saw the wreck someone had made of the room her face went pale.

"Oh, goodness," she said, her body sagging as she leaned against the wall. "I can't take all of this. My constitution is just too delicate." She gazed at McNab. "You should leave. You've been threatened!"

"Don't get all worked up," McNab said hurriedly. "Everything will be fine."

"That's right." Maxim put a hand on her shoulder. "It might be some sort of prank. Apparently there is a disgruntled worker lurking about. It seems he's angry, but we don't think he's dangerous."

Was he forgetting that he might have been responsible for the chandelier falling down? the twins wondered. Someone could have gotten hurt, although no one could be sure that it hadn't been an accident. Maybe Maxim was just trying to calm Ms. Esposito.

"We'll get to the bottom of this," Aunt Edith said hurriedly. "Don't worry, Muriel. I tend to agree with Maxim. It's a prank."

"I'm going to go splash some cold water on my face," said McNab. He walked into the bathroom and let out a yell. "In the toilet! It's a huge rat, and it's trying to jump out!"

Nobody moved. They all hated rats.

"Aw, why does there have to be a problem in a toilet again?" Cody mumbled. "Come on, Otis. Let's have a look." They headed cautiously into the bathroom.

The rat in the toilet was a super-gruesome sight. The animal looked crazed. It was a dark gray with a pointed snout. There was blood around its mouth and growling sounds erupted from it as it tried to jump again and again but kept losing its footing on the smooth porcelain.

"Eww . . . gross," said Otis. "Maybe it has rabies. And there's no way to get it out of there without getting bitten, right? If we just leave it alone it will tire itself out and drown."

"How did it get in here anyhow?" Cody wondered aloud.

Other guests appeared. They had returned to the inn for lunch and then heard the commotion.

"Now, you boys be careful," Eric Barber said in a shaky voice. "I think you should stay away from that awful animal."

"Yeah, I think you're right," Otis agreed. "Come on, Cody, there's nothing we can do."

But Cody didn't move. He stood still, head tilted, staring at the rat. Then, before anyone could stop him, his hand shot out and he grabbed the rat's head.

Everyone gasped and groaned. Some were too shocked to make a sound. They just stared, unable to believe what they had just seen. Cody held onto the rat tightly as it thrashed.

"I think I'm going to be sick," murmured Mr. Barber.

"Me, too," said Ms. Wallace.

Muriel Esposito had pressed her hand to her mouth.

"It's okay, folks, really," said Cody. He held up the thrashing rat by the tail to convince them. It didn't work. It just sent everyone into more spasms of horror.

Cody shook the dripping rat. Its movements were slowing down.

"It's not real," he said. "It's a fake . . . a toy. Look!" He peeled back a flap of fur on the rat's stomach and exposed a black switch. He flicked it and the rat was suddenly still.

Everyone gasped. "But . . . how did you know?" Ms. Wallace's voice trailed off.

Cody shrugged. "Back home I sometimes help out in a store called Wackorama. They sell a lot of goofy gadgets like whoopee cushions and hand buzzers. Fake rats are one of our most popular items around Halloween. I guess a fake rat makes a great *party booby trap*," he said, giving his brother a sidelong glance.

Otis rolled his eyes and nodded back to let his brother know he recognized the palindrome.

"That thing is disgusting," said Ms. Esposito.

"I know," Cody agreed.

"I can't take it anymore," said Aunt Edith. "I'm calling the police."

✳

All of the guests were gathered in the front hall when Officer Tano arrived. They followed as Aunt Edith took him to McNab's room. The officer examined the mess, the mechanical rat, and the note.

He treated the whole thing as a joke. He talked to Aunt Edith as if she were a child.

"You got me out here for this, lady?" he asked with a smirk. "This is the kind of thing the local kids do. They know that you're new to the island, and they decided to have some fun with you."

"Well, maybe this is your idea of fun, but it isn't mine," said McNab.

"It isn't mine, either," said Maxim. "Frankly, I'm shocked by your reaction."

The police officer's smirk deepened. "Messing up a room, putting a toy in the toilet, and leaving a note . . . is that what you call a real crime? I don't." He turned to McNab. "Was anything stolen?"

"Well, no, there wasn't," McNab admitted.

"See? This was some kind of kid's prank," said Officer Tano.

"What about the worker I told you about on the phone?" asked Aunt Edith. "The one I fired?"

"We can't prove it was him," the officer said smoothly. He smiled broadly at the guests. "Go on about your business, everybody. There was no crime here."

As Officer Tano drove away, the guests began muttering. Strangely enough, the officer's unconcerned attitude was catching. As they began leaving, several guests were shrugging and mumbling about pranks.

"Unbelievable, just unbelievable," said Aunt Edith. "That man didn't take this seriously at all."

"That was really weird," Cody said to Otis as they walked downstairs.

"Yeah," Otis agreed. "What Aunt Edith said about firing that worker adds another suspect. I wonder how we can find out about this guy."

"We'll ask the gardener," said Cody. "He's been on the island his whole life. Maybe he knows something."

They headed out to the garden to find Winston Cato.

[Chapter Nine]

Winston Cato wasn't difficult to find. He was singing as he trimmed the hedges.

"*He'll* know something about the guy who got fired, if anybody does," said Otis.

The boys walked over and stood beside the gardener.

"When you've got a minute, Mr. Cato, we'd like to ask you something," said Cody.

Cato kept on cutting for a moment. Then he put down his shears and mopped his brow. "What is it, boys?" he asked. "I notice that you are curious about many things. You really watch what's going on. You try to figure things out." Cato's eyes twinkled. His words surprised both of the boys. They had been so busy watching others that they never thought about being watched themselves. They hoped that they weren't the *only* ones Cato watched.

"We were wondering about one of the men who worked on renovating the inn," Otis said. "Did you know the guy who got fired?"

"Oh, uh-huh, that one. He was something, all right."

"Something? What do you mean?" asked Cody.

"He was up to something, that one. Always walking around when he was supposed to be working."

"Where did he go?" Otis asked.

Cato shrugged. "I don't know. *I* was working," he said. "But I'd see him going here and there. He was always smiling, always happy, like he was laughing at a joke of his own."

"Wasn't he angry that he got fired?" asked Cody.

"Yeah, did he talk about getting revenge?" asked Otis.

"Angry? No, he wasn't angry. In fact, he laughed about it. He said the timing was perfect. He said that soon he was going to have all the money he needed. Isn't that strange? A guy who just got fired talking about having lots of money?"

"It sure is," Otis agreed.

"What did this guy look like?" Cody asked.

Cato looked thoughtful. "He was about average height, with dark coloring, brown hair, and a mustache and beard. His eyebrows were kind of bushy. He called himself Kendall."

Otis brushed a mosquito off his arm. "So, um, do you see this guy around much?"

"Nah—he left the island."

"Are you sure?" Cody asked, his heart sinking. If the man really had left the island then someone else was causing the trouble.

Cato waved a hand in the air. "Oh, sure. Listen, I know everybody on this island, especially people who work in construction and gardening. That's because we often work together. That guy left the island, for sure . . . unless he's hiding under a rock."

Cody had a thought. "If you know everybody on the island, you probably know the woman who was cooking at the inn."

A shadow seemed to cross Cato's face. "Aida. Yes, I know her, but not very well."

"Do you know why she left?" Cody asked.

Cato pressed his lips into a thin line. "She said she was scared to stay around here. She told me that she was afraid of the pirate's ghost, but . . ." He shrugged.

"You weren't sure she was telling the truth, were you?" Otis asked.

Cato shrugged again. "Well, I don't know for sure. I've got my own ideas, though."

"Such as what?" Cody asked. "A lot of people think the place is haunted, don't they?"

"Yes, but no one on the island was afraid. The ghost has been around forever. He never hurt anyone." Cato ran a hand through his jet-black hair and laughed. "I don't think that ghost is very smart. He's been looking for his treasure for years and *still* hasn't found it."

He looked at the boys for a moment and scratched his head. "You know, I don't want to spoil anything for you two. But since your aunt bought the inn it's been a lot more haunted than usual."

"Huh?" Cody and Otis both said together.

Cato took a deep breath and shook his head. "You guys are old enough to know the truth. Your aunt has been *making* some of the hauntings. She hired a company that creates special effects for the movies. They were here for a whole week installing a sound system and projectors . . . all kinds of stuff."

"See, I *knew* ghosts weren't real," Otis said with satisfaction.

Cody's shoulders sagged.

"Wait a minute," said Cato. "I didn't say the place wasn't haunted. It *is*. I just meant that your aunt was adding to the excitement. She wanted to make sure that everyone got a chance to see and hear the ghost. She figured it would be good for business. The real one is still around, though. He was here long before your aunt arrived."

"What about the guide? Why did *he* leave?" Cody asked.

Cato shook his head. "The guide didn't give me a reason. He just said he was getting out. Look, everybody who worked here knew your aunt was creating her own ghost. But don't spoil things for the guests. They're sure they're in a real haunted inn. Real ghosts aren't as reliable as manufactured ones."

"We don't want to spoil the fun," said Otis. "But if the cook and the guide weren't afraid of the ghost, why did they leave the inn? I'm sure my aunt paid them well."

A cloud of butterflies flew by, their wings all shades of blue, red, yellow, orange, and pink. Cato watched them for a moment. Then he cleared his throat.

"Maybe someone else paid them more money to leave," he said. "I used to see things around here at night—boats coming and going."

Cato looked into the distance. Then he gave himself a shake. "I talk too much sometimes," he said. "This is nothing you boys should worry about. People leave jobs all the time. Just enjoy the beautiful island."

He put his gloves back on and picked up his hedge

clippers. "Silly me," he mumbled, "talking nonsense to a couple of boys. Forget what I said. Run along now."

✱

"That was weird," said Otis when he and Cody were back in their room after lunch. "Cato was doing a lot of talking. Then he got kind of spacey."

Otis was standing beside his bed, his back to the wall. Cody was in front of him, bent down under his own bed. He was looking for his sneakers.

"Do you think somebody paid the cook and the guide to leave, Otis?"

Cody waited a moment. Otis didn't answer.

"I think somebody doesn't want the inn to stay in business," Cody went on. "It's hard to figure out. That guy Cordell definitely seems to want people to be scared of the place. And he and Sam Keller are up to something. Why isn't Cordell going by his real name? Didn't that officer Tano seem strange, too? Imagine a police officer who treats everything like a big joke."

Cody waited for his brother to jump in with thoughts of his own. When he didn't, Cody went on talking . . . and talking . . . and talking. "I can't find my sneakers," he mumbled several minutes later. "Have you seen them anywhere, Otis?"

When Otis didn't reply, Cody got up and turned around. "Why don't you answer me? You haven't said a word."

Cody found himself talking to a blank wall. His jaw dropped. Otis was gone.

[Chapter Ten]

Cody heard a pounding behind the wall. "Cody! Cody! I'm in here! Get me out!" It was Otis.

"Well, how did you get in there?"

"I don't know. I must have hit a button or lever or something. The wall slid back and I fell into this secret compartment."

"Wow. What's back there?"

"It's just a sort of crawl space. It's just a slot behind the wall."

"Maybe it was the pirate's hiding place."

"Maybe. Will you stop talking and get me out of here?!"

"Oh, sorry . . . okay, okay." Cody's eyes began searching the wall. His hands felt for a seam. The wall was smooth, with dark baseboard paneling.

There were carvings in the baseboard—flowers. But then hidden among the flowers was a skull. Cody sucked in his breath when he saw it, then pressed his finger to its surface.

Swoosh! A panel in the wall slid back a few inches, then sideways to reveal Otis standing there, his face red and his hair dishevelled.

Wooo! He exhaled a puff of air as he stepped into the room. "It was hot in there and dark. How'd you open up the panel?"

Otis pointed to the skull and then pressed it. The panel slid back into place.

"Awesome," said Otis. "Thanks." He took a deep breath.

"Well, I didn't want to have to hack up Aunt Edith's wall," Cody said, slapping his brother on the back.

"I think it's more than just a hiding place," said Otis. "The wall behind me sounded hollow. We should see if we can open that inside panel. We'll get some flashlights and—"

Rae burst into the room. "You've got to come downstairs! You're not going to believe who just came to the inn! Oh, this is amazing!" She turned her back and ran out.

Cody and Otis looked at each other for a moment. Otis shrugged. "Well, I guess we ought to go see who it is."

They headed for the staircase. Sam Keller was already halfway down. "Hey!" he called to a tall, muscular man wearing red shorts and a gray T-shirt. The man looked at him and his mouth opened slightly. He closed it quickly, frowned, and shook his head slightly.

Rae was hovering over someone with short, dark hair who was sitting with his back to her. She was smiling but looked slightly dazed.

The boys reached the bottom of the stairs a few steps behind Keller, who was walking over to introduce himself. He stuck out his hand and the tall, muscular man shook it.

"Sam Keller."

"Ronnie Walker."

"It looked like they recognized each other before," Cody whispered to his brother. "But now they act like they're seeing each other for the first time."

"Right," Otis agreed. "Now, who is the other guy?"

Just then the other guy stood up. Cody and Otis both gasped.

Jamal Mason gave the boys a sour look and then turned to Ronnie Walker. "What kind of bodyguard are you, anyway? I thought you said only *old* people were going to be here," the young movie star said sullenly. "I don't want fans bugging me while I'm on vacation."

Walker shrugged. "Sorry, Jamal. I didn't know about the kids."

Cody and Otis both scowled and stuffed their hands in their pockets. Neither one liked the way he said "kids"—as if they ought to be in a nursery. But Rae looked as if she hadn't heard a word. She was gazing at Jamal.

"I like your wristband, Jamal," she said.

Jamal favored her with a grudging half-smile. He held up his arm to show an elaborately woven wristband of many colors.

"A friend of mine just gave this to me. It's Egyptian," he said, "and it's really old. He found it in a box in a cave. This guy worked with a museum and knows about ancient artifacts. He said it's probably from about 1300 BC—maybe even older."

"Awesome," said Rae. "But shouldn't something like that really be in a museum, because—"

Jamal cut her off. "Oh, mind your own business," he said rudely. He turned to Walker and said, "Take care of the check-in. I'm going for a walk." He shook his head and muttered, "I don't know about this place. Maybe I should go over to the next island. It's hipper on Tacayno."

By now, Ms. Wallace and Mr. Barber had appeared in the lobby. They had observed the scene. So had Mr. McNab, who had been reading a book in the corner, near a sour-faced Mr. Cordell.

"That young man should be taught a lesson about manners," Mr. McNab said in a surprisingly dark tone.

"How right you are," echoed Ms. Wallace, as Mr. Barber nodded in agreement.

Mr. Cordell got to his feet. "I'm going for a walk on the beach," he announced. He looked at Mr. Keller. "Wanna join me?" he said, in a tone that was more like an instruction than a question.

Rae still looked stunned. "I'm going to find Jamal," she said, then hurried outside.

Cody and Otis exchanged glances. Rae must be starstruck—she definitely had a crush on Jamal. Still, it wasn't like her to put up with rude behavior, even from Jamal Mason. But they had something else to worry about right now. They hurried after Ronnie Walker, who was waiting at the check-in desk.

They found him there, pacing back and forth, muttering to himself. They caught snatches of speech.

"That's right—teach him a lesson . . . show him . . . find out . . ."

"Excuse me, Mr. Walker . . ." Cody began. "We

noticed that Sam Keller seemed to know you . . . and then he didn't."

Color flooded into Mr. Walker's face, turning it a bright pink. "Oh, the guy with the crazy red hair and the weird tattoo? Well, we met about six years ago—but just briefly. I've worked out a lot since then—I guess I wasn't sure whether he recognized me or not." He shrugged and turned away.

"Hey, what do you kids care about it, anyway?" he asked over his shoulder, sounding annoyed. "Why don't you go play some games or something?"

Cody's eyes flashed. He opened his mouth to say something but Otis put a hand on his arm and shook his head. He held a finger to his lips and then said, "You're right, sir. We'll just go do that."

When they had walked a few yards away, Otis said, "No sense ticking him off. We want to find out what game *he's* playing."

"Yeah, I think what he said was lame. It looks like Sam Keller makes some dumb mistakes, like calling Steve Cordell 'Jimmy,'" Otis said.

Just then Rae came striding toward them. Her eyes blazed and her mouth was set in a thin line.

"That Jamal Mason has a head the size of a watermelon, he's so full of himself," she said. "I tried to talk to him and he told me to get lost. He said the inn was a dump and that coming to this island was a stupid idea. So I told him he was a spoiled brat and I was never going to see one of his movies again."

"Well, you're back to your old self anyway." Cody laughed.

"So much for our favorite movie star," grumbled Otis. "What a downer that he's so stuck-up."

"Yeah," Rae sighed. "He thinks he's all that and a bag of chips." She sighed again.

"Well, cheer up. We think we've found a secret passage. Maybe it will give us some clues to the mystery."

Rae wrinkled her nose. "That's cool," she said, "but I'm here for a vacation. Anyway, what do you mean you *think* you found one?"

The twins told her about the sliding panel and the hiding place. "Maybe there's a secret passage behind the second wall," said Cody.

"Well, good luck, guys. I'm heading back to the beach. Swimming is the only thing that will cheer me up."

The twins watched her walk away. Cody scratched his head. "Who wouldn't want to find a secret passage?"

"Yeah," Otis agreed. "I wish we could get Rae

more into mysteries. She'd really be a help in finding clues."

Cody nodded. "She sure would. But she's just not interested. I don't get it."

Otis agreed. "Well, maybe she'll come around. Anyway, let's go find that secret passage."

[Chapter Eleven]

Back in their room, the boys pocketed their pen-lights. They opened the panel and searched for more skull buttons. They quickly located two more—one that opened the panel from the inside. A third opened the second wall from the other side. Now that they were sure they could get out, they were ready to explore.

They stepped through the second opening and found a set of steps, at the bottom of which was a winding tunnel. It was lined with bricks that seemed very old. The mortar between them was dark and crumbling.

Soon, however, the scene changed. The twins walked into a smooth, modern hallway with freshly painted walls and modern light fixtures. Then they came to a series of rooms.

They listened for voices as they stepped inside one

room after another. What they found made their hearts pound and their heads spin.

There were boxes and boxes and stacks and stacks of DVDs. A quick check revealed that many were movies they had heard of—movies that had just been released to theaters.

They also found several computers, camcorders, and other equipment. *They're burning DVDs here*, the twins realized. *Lots and lots of them.*

"We've got real modern-day pirates selling pirated DVDs," Cody whispered.

"Yeah," Otis said, "someone is doing a big business. The inn must be getting in the way."

It looked as if the business had been going on for a while, and the plan was for it to go on longer. One of the rooms in the secret passage was outfitted with couches, a pool table, a kitchen, and a huge flat-screen television. *The crooks must view their DVDs here*, Otis thought.

In another room was a row of single beds. There was even an office. Everything had been chosen for maximum comfort. It looked like a high-class underground hotel.

They turned around and began heading back. When they reached the bottom of the stairs, they heard men talking. The sound was coming from somewhere behind them. They knew those voices. It was Steve Cordell and Sam Keller.

*

Back in their room, beads of sweat dotting their foreheads, the boys watched as the secret panel slid back into place. They both exhaled sighs of relief.

"I'll bet Black Heart the pirate originally made that tunnel," Cody said. His eyes danced with excitement.

"Probably," Otis agreed. "But somebody else is using it now."

"We'd better go find Dad, Maxim, and Aunt Edith and tell them what's going on," said Cody. He turned to leave the room.

"Wait! There is more to this than just DVDs. We've got to find out who these guys are. Let's get something on them that they can't lie their way out of."

"Oh, there you go talking about lying again. We've got a pile of bootleg DVDs and burner equipment under the inn. They can't lie their way out of that. This is something out of our league, Otis. We can't be detectives here. We need *real* detectives."

"We can't prove that it was Cordell and Keller we heard. And who is Cordell, really? I think we should search his room and find out."

"Break into his room? Are you nuts?"

"It's our aunt's place, Cody. He's carrying on crimes in our aunt's inn."

Cody crossed his arms. "What if he catches us?"

"He's down there in the secret passage. I'll bet we can get in and out really fast. Let's find out who this guy is. He's probably the one who is giving Aunt Edith so much trouble . . . along with his buddy Sam Keller."

[Chapter Twelve]

"We shouldn't be doing this," said Cody.

"I know," Otis whispered as he glanced nervously over his shoulder. He bent down in front of the door to Steve Cordell's room and took a video-store membership card from his pocket. "I think we have to do it, though. He's committing a crime in our aunt's place. We have to find out what he's up to."

"Can you really get in with that thing?" asked Cody.

Otis jiggled the card carefully. "Yeah, I'm pretty sure I can. These locks aren't exactly state of the art. I don't think Aunt Edith figured on having any thieves in the place."

"We're not thieves!" Cody whispered urgently.

Otis glanced up at him. "Come on, Cody, get a grip. I didn't mean *we* were thieves."

"Okay, okay . . . but that's what we'd look like if we got caught."

"We won't get caught." Otis jiggled the card again.

"Wait a minute! I think I hear somebody."

Both boys froze and held their breath. Silence.

"You're getting all wired, Cody. Calm down." Otis gave the card a little push and turned the knob. "Got it," he mumbled as the door swung open.

"Remember, leave everything exactly as it is— and don't break anything!" Cody said hurriedly as he tiptoed into the room.

"Well, our pal's a slob," said Otis with a chuckle. There were socks and shirts tumbled over the floor and a jacket flung on a chair along with two rumpled pairs of pants.

"Who cares? We're here trying to find out if he's a criminal," Cody muttered as he pulled open a dresser drawer. He pawed gingerly through a pile of T-shirts. After a moment he closed the drawer and opened the next one.

Otis was searching through the desk. "This is weird," he said as he picked up a couple of magazines. "*Casino King, Slots, Bluffer, Lucky, Rowdy Roulette . . .* These are all gambling magazines. What's a guy who likes gambling doing in a place like this?"

Cody shrugged. "Saving money?" He opened another drawer.

"Keep looking," Otis told him. "I'll check the closet while you finish the desk."

"Maybe I've found something," Otis announced moments later. "Cordell wrote a note on this pad. The note itself is gone but maybe I can find out what it said."

Cordell's writing had left an impression on the blank surface of the notepad. Otis tore off a blank sheet from the back of the pad and laid it over the top sheet. Then he grabbed a pencil and rubbed the side of the lead gently across the surface. Letters and numbers appeared.

"It's just some kind of list of personal expenses," he said, disappointment in his voice. He began reading them aloud: "Haircuts, $100; suits, $900; car repair, $250; casino, $4,000; tan $5,000; massages, $450 . . . This guy likes to spend, and he's vain." He chuckled. "That's a lot of tanning—like, a year's worth at least. But the letters look the same as those jagged ones on the note in McNab's room."

He stuffed the piece of paper into his pocket. "How are you doing over there?"

Cody was looking through the closet. "I've found his wallet in a jacket," he said, holding it up. He began fumbling through the contents. The more he looked, the more his gut twisted.

"This guy isn't who he says he is, that's for sure." Cody examined the credit card in his hand, replaced it, and withdrew another, then a driver's license. "He's got credit cards under two different names and a driver's license under a third name. Jacob Netter, Frank Marks, Martin Rathbone. None of the names is Steve Cordell."

Otis frowned as he rifled through a drawer. "Stolen cards? Or aliases?" His heart beat faster as he laid eyes on a passport. His hands shook as he opened it. "His passport says Martin Rathbone. So what does this all—"

Suddenly Otis's fast-beating heart began racing. He looked at his brother. All color had drained from his face. He mouthed the words, "Someone's coming."

Cody nodded as the footsteps drew closer and closer. He pointed under the bed.

Otis shoved the passport back into the drawer. He clenched his teeth as he closed the drawer without making a sound.

The footsteps stopped. The doorknob began to turn. Both boys dove to the floor and rolled.

They peered from under the bed and saw scuffed sneakers step into the room, followed by a pair of flip-flops on pale feet.

Both twins felt the sweat begin trickling down

their faces. Cody and Otis dared not move a muscle. Every minute seemed to last forever.

"Look, your plan isn't working," one of the men said. The twins recognized Sam Keller's voice. He sounded exasperated.

"There isn't much more we can do." Steve Cordell's voice was an angry snarl.

"Of course there is," Keller snapped. "Quit fooling around with this kiddie stuff. It's not *really* scaring anyone. You're afraid to get tough," he taunted.

Now Cordell's voice sneered. "Yeah, what do you have in mind, genius?"

Keller snorted. "Maybe have a talk with Edith the way I did with her cook." He snorted again. "We should do whatever it takes, even if we have to burn the place down. Hey, that would get rid of these people." Keller actually laughed.

"Oh, those are real smart ideas. It's a lucky thing that cook didn't go running to the police after you threatened her. That's just what the Boss doesn't want—the police sniffing around here. That's all we need. And how can you even think about burning the place down with all our *pirate treasure* here?"

Otis and Cody looked at each other. So these two men were responsible for all the "accidents."

"Okay, so we can't burn the place down," Keller said grudgingly. "How are we going to take care of business? Everything will get screwed up and both of us will be in hot water with the Boss." Keller's hand slapped a wall. "It's dangerous to get on the wrong side of that guy."

"Oh, come on, calm down. Take it easy." The twins heard Cordell cracking his knuckles. "I wish I'd never taken a job with that guy. The money's good, but he's always in our faces. I've got to admit, it's a sweet deal, though. We carry the stuff right through the tunnel, load it on the boat, and go out to sea."

Cody was trying to remain calm, but he was having a hard time. Moments before, he had inhaled some dust. Now a sneeze threatened. It was getting closer by the second.

Otis watched as his brother's face turned from pink to red. He bit his lip. Whatever Cody was trying to do, he prayed he could do it.

Cody squeezed his eyes shut and gritted his teeth. The sneeze kept building. He began moving his arm ever so slowly. His muscles were so tense that they ached. Finally he was able to press a finger firmly under his nose. He stopped the sneeze just as it surged from inside.

Both twins would have sighed with relief had they dared. But they couldn't risk being heard. What happened next nearly made them gasp in surprise.

Steve Cordell sat down on the bed, making the springs creak. The twins each prayed that he wasn't planning on taking a nap.

But he was only changing his shoes. He kicked off the scuffed sneakers and grabbed a pair of sandals.

"Listen, little brother," he said. "You always worried too much even when we were kids. You used to drive yourself nuts worrying if you'd pass a test or make the team or get caught stealing change from Mom's purse. Everything always turned out okay. This will, too. We'll figure everything out. It'll be fine. Once this *big job* is finished, we'll be on easy street."

The twins felt a jolt when they heard the word "brother." Cordell and Keller, or whatever their real names were, were brothers! Keller wasn't who he claimed to be, either. Now it was easy to understand why they were concealing their identities. That's what criminals did.

"I want to get everything done right away. This isn't like stealing nickels and dimes," Keller replied. "This is big money . . . or big trouble. The kind of trouble that really hurts and doesn't go away. The kind of trouble you can't talk your way out of. The kind of trouble that—"

"Knock it off!" Cordell yelled. Then it sounded like he punched his palm with his fist. "Keep it up and you'll get me worrying, too." He let out a long sigh. "Look, when you worry too much, you make mistakes. That's no good. Just keep your mind on business. Remember, you're Sam Keller, and do your job. We'll figure out what to do about the inn later. Just focus."

Cordell heaved himself off the bed. "Come on, bro'. Let's go down to the beach, lie on the sand, play some cards, relax."

"Okay, maybe that's what I need," Keller said slowly. Then he spit out his next sentence. "But I sure would like to be rid of those three smart-aleck kids."

Cody felt the skin on the back of his neck tighten. A shiver ran up Otis's spine. This guy sounded like he was losing it.

"Now you're worried about a couple of kids? What am I going to do with you? Come on, let's go make like we're guests soaking up the sun."

At last, the two men left. When the door closed

behind them, Cody and Otis went limp. They waited several minutes before dragging themselves out from under the bed and struggling to their feet. "That was too close," said Otis as he mopped his forehead with the edge of his shirt. "I'm sweating so much I'm surprised they couldn't smell me."

"Tell me about it," Cody agreed. He sat down where Cordell had been moments before. "Well, now we know they're up to more than selling pirated DVDs for sure. But we have no idea what it is."

"I wish I could remember where I saw that guy who calls himself Cordell before." Otis bit his lip. "Too bad that we're on our own," he said. "It's not like we can tell anyone what we found. We can't exactly tell Dad or Maxim or Aunt Edith that we broke into someone's room and went through his wallet."

"Even if we found credit cards with different names, and that Cordell and Keller are brothers?" Cody asked. Then he answered his own question. "No, we can't. It's just not enough. Two slick guys like them would deny everything, and then nobody would insist on seeing the passport and credit cards. Maxim and Dad think we're playing detective anyhow."

"Right," Otis agreed. "We need more proof. What's this *big job* they were talking about?"

Cody put his ear to the door. "I don't hear anything. Let's get out of here."

He opened the door slowly and peered into the hallway. "All clear," he said. "Let's go."

Cody and Otis exited the room and strode briskly toward their own. Inside, Cody looked at his brother thoughtfully.

"I've got to admit that you were right about breaking into that guy's room," he said. "We never would have found out all that stuff if we hadn't."

"Uh-huh," Otis agreed. "Now we just have to figure out what to do next."

They went downstairs and found Aunt Edith behind the check-in desk, staring into space, her shoulders sagging. She looked worried and upset. The twins exchanged glances.

"What's the matter, Aunt Edith?" Cody asked.

"Can we help?" asked Otis.

Aunt Edith looked up and smiled. "Thank you, boys, but I don't think so. I don't know what's going on around here, but it isn't good. Muriel Esposito checked out a little while ago. She said she didn't feel safe here. And then Inez, the maid, left just now. She said it was dangerous to stay. This place could be wonderful but it's falling apart around me."

"Well, I think we can help after all, Aunt Edith," Cody said with a smile. "Otis and I can be your new cleaning crew."

"Rae will help, too," said Otis. "I know she'll want to."

Aunt Edith's face brightened. "Well, that's a wonderful idea. Thank you, boys, and I'll have to thank Rae, too. You *are* a help."

"Otis is a slob, but maybe he'll be good at cleaning up other people's messes." Cody chuckled.

Otis punched him in the arm. "You should talk, pigpen."

"I believe you both will do very well," said Aunt Edith with a smile.

Then suddenly the smile vanished. "Don't tell anyone that Inez left yet," she said seriously. "Anyone except Rae, of course. They'll find out, but I just don't want to make a big deal about it. There are enough people leaving this place already."

They both agreed not to say anything and to ask Rae to do the same.

She handed them some duplicate room keys. "Be careful not to lose these," she said, shaking a pointed finger at them. "We don't have a locksmith on this island."

"We'll be careful, Aunt Edith. Don't worry," Cody told her.

As they walked along the beach to tell Rae the plan, Otis held up a key and grinned. "Now we won't have to break into another room."

"Like Sam Keller's." Cody nodded.

"Like Sam Keller's."

[Chapter Thirteen]

Late that night, when everyone had gone to sleep, a scream shattered the silence. Lights were turned on quickly and the guests ran to find out what happened.

Helen Wallace was standing in her doorway. She was in her robe and had a towel wrapped around her head.

"I was getting ready to shower when I heard a noise," she said. "I came out of the bathroom and the room was dark. He was there—the ghost! He was sort of . . . glowing. He was dressed in a pirate costume and he was carrying a sword and mumbling about treasure. Then he told me he knew I was planning to steal it and if I tried to take it, he'd kill me! He said I'd better leave this place!"

McNab hurried to her side. "Don't be afraid, Ms. Wallace. We've all heard the ghost and he hasn't harmed anyone." He tried to take her hand.

She pulled away. "Don't you touch me!" Her eyes narrowed. "Was it you? Was this some stunt to scare me off?"

McNab stared at her. "Why would I try to do that? You're very upset, Ms. Wallace, or you wouldn't say such a thing. It's all right, though, I understand."

Ms. Wallace stamped her foot. "There's something *really* strange going on," she said. "Anybody'd be crazy to stay here!" She slammed her door.

"We've got to have a talk with Aunt Edith," Otis said when the twins were back in their room. "These hauntings of hers won't promote business—they'll kill it . . . for real. What was she thinking with this latest trick?"

"Maybe it wasn't a trick," said Cody. "We know it wasn't Cordell or Keller. They were already at Ms. Wallace's door when we arrived. That means they got there moments after she screamed. Neither one had time to change out of a costume and into pajamas."

"Aw, don't start with that pirate ghost again," Otis said, jumping under the covers. "You know what bothers me? She said she was getting ready to get into the shower . . . but she had a towel around her head. Why? Wouldn't she put the towel around her hair *after the shower*?"

Cody sat down on his bed. "You're right." He thought for a minute. "What if she made up the whole story? What if she screamed and talked about the ghost to scare *other* people away from the inn?"

"Yeah . . . but why?"

Cody shrugged. "Maybe she wants to buy it."

The next morning they found their aunt before breakfast. They told her what they had learned from Winston Cato.

"What made you put together a trick like that, Aunt Edith? Do you really think it's good for business?"

"Don't you tell anyone I was engineering some—most—of those hauntings!"

"We won't, but you can't do things like you did last night," said Cody.

Aunt Edith put her hands on her hips and looked down. "I didn't," she said. "I'd already decided to stop faking the hauntings. Then *that* happened."

The twins stared back at her with eyes like saucers. "You ought to call the police again. Even if someone just wanted to scare her, they *broke into her room*."

Aunt Edith held up a hand. "Hold on, boys. I've already talked to Helen Wallace. She said she thought it over and realized she'd left her door open. She also said she knew who was disguised as the ghost."

"Who?" they both asked at once.

"She wouldn't tell me. All she would say was that it was a personal vendetta and nothing dangerous."

That left them speechless. So did the sight of Ms. Wallace with bright red hair instead of her brown bob at breakfast.

"I just decided I needed a change!" she said. "I had the hair color with me but I couldn't make up my mind whether to use it or not—until last night."

"Hair color explains the towel on her head before showering," Rae said after breakfast. "I'd been wondering about it."

"So were we," said Otis. "I don't know much about hair color. Can you explain?"

Rae nodded. "My mom colors her hair and rinses out the color in the sink before she takes a shower. See? It makes sense."

Cody frowned. "But I still wonder who pulled the haunting."

"Well, let's get started on our cleaning," said Otis.

*

"I'm more nervous than I was when we broke into Cordell's," Cody told his brother. "If we have to hide again, I don't think I can take it."

"We won't have to hide. We didn't break in. We're supposed to be here."

"We're supposed to be cleaning and you and I both know that's not why we're really here," said Cody. "Let's just get this over with."

They unlocked Keller's room and headed inside. Otis let out a whistle.

"There won't be much cleaning to do in here," he said.

He was right. Sam Keller's room was as neat as his brother's was sloppy. A look inside the dresser drawers revealed nothing but neatly folded clothes. Cody checked the pockets of the jackets and pants in the closet and found nothing.

"I don't see his wallet or passport in the desk," said Otis.

"I'll try the nightstand."

Cody came up empty. "I guess Keller, or whoever he is, is the kind of guy who keeps all his IDs on him. I guess I might as well try the bathroom."

"Well, this guy likes gambling magazines, too," Otis said. "And I found a couple of poker chips with the logo of a Las Vegas hotel. Cordell mentioned playing cards. . . . It looks like these guys are a couple of gamblers."

"Gambling in Las Vegas isn't a crime, though," Cody whispered. He opened the doors to the cabinet under the bathroom sink. He pulled out a rectangular plastic case and unzipped it. He sucked in his breath when he saw what was inside.

There were two wigs, one brown and one gray, a couple of mustaches of different sizes, a couple of beards, and a pair of bushy eyebrows, plus several tubes of makeup. A bottle of self-tanner was beside several contact lens cases that held lenses of brown, hazel, green, and gray.

Cody hurriedly rezipped the case and replaced it in the cabinet. He walked over to where Otis was peering underneath the bed. "Our guy is into disguises," he said.

Otis pulled a newspaper from under the bed and sat back on his heels, studying a photo on the page in front of him. His eyes widened.

"He likes to save souvenirs, too," he said. "This paper is from a few days ago." He held up the section of *The Las Vegas Star*. "Check out the photo. It's another casino party—like the one that was in the paper Maxim was reading before we left. There's that gangster at the party. His name is Moe Kleese. Check out a couple of his friends in the background. Look really close."

Cody looked at the photo. At first he didn't know what Otis was talking about, but then he saw it. Just beyond the gangster's shoulder stood Steve Cordell.

"Here's another one." Otis handed him another newspaper with a photo of the group. It was dated six years earlier. This time Keller had brown hair.

"Remember that worker Aunt Edith said she had to fire? The one with the brown hair and mustache, the dark eyes, and the bushy eyebrows? Keller has to be our man," said Cody.

"It looks like he made sure things would go wrong at the inn." Otis nodded. "They made a plan to scare people off the island before Aunt Edith even opened the place." He ran a hand through his hair.

"So the inn is interfering with their business, whatever that is," Cody went on. "Shutting it down is important. Important enough to cause accidents and scare people—but nothing bad enough to attract the attention of the police . . . at least, not major attention."

Otis was nodding. "And the officer who shows up when something gets reported never takes it seriously. He acts like it's all a big joke." He pulled out the note paper he'd taken from Cordell's room and waved it. "What do you think?"

"I think we've figured it out. He wasn't paying for a phony tan in installments. He was making payments to *Tano* at $5,000 every month," said Cody. "Tano was paid off."

He chewed his lower lip and frowned. "Whatever Cordell and Keller are tangled up in, it's important enough to approach a police officer and pay him off. Otis, I think we're in over our heads. We should get someone to help us. This seems really dangerous."

Otis sighed. "You're right. But we still don't have enough evidence to convince anyone that they are crooks. So Keller has some disguises? Maybe it's a hobby. He has an old newspaper? So what?"

"We've got passports with fake names. We've got a basement full of pirated DVDs," said Cody.

"Come on, we can do better. What's this *big job*? We need more evidence. If we don't get it, they'll keep trying to close the inn. They'll keep doing whatever it is. But we've got to be careful, and make sure they don't suspect us."

"Okay," Cody agreed after a moment. "Let's get out of here and—"

A thundering roar filled the air. It was coming from down the hall. The twins raced to see what had happened.

[Chapter Fourteen]

They found Rae standing at the door of Albert McNab's room. "What were you doing in my room?" he thundered.

"Cleaning it," Rae s aid calmly, looking him in the eye.

"Cleaning it?" McNab sputtered.

"Well, someone has to," she said.

"I didn't think anyone would be in the room since the maid left," he said, calming down. "I was just surprised, that's all." He smiled slightly.

Eric Barber and Helen Wallace appeared. McNab scowled when he saw them.

"What is it, Mr. McNab? Bad news about your *grocery business*?"

"You two," he muttered. "No, it isn't about my grocery business. But why don't you mind your *own business*? And quit shadowing me."

Cody and Otis exchanged glances. "How did you know Inez was gone?"

McNab glared at them. "She *told* me *herself.* Yesterday. She said she got a new job that paid better. So I didn't expect anyone in my room. Rae startled me." His voice softened. "I'm sorry I yelled."

"I guess you really were surprised," said Rae, who was shocked that McNab had acted the way he had. He was usually so charming.

"What's all the commotion?" asked Steve Cordell, who had Sam Keller at his elbow. He peered into McNab's room.

"Confound it," said McNab. "Why is everybody so interested in my room?"

"Can I just finish cleaning it?" asked Rae.

"Uh—no, dear, that won't be necessary." McNab gently guided Rae from the room and stepped inside. "I'll take care of it until a new maid arrives."

"*If* one arrives," snorted Cordell. "I think this place is getting a reputation."

Suddenly he shot a threatening look at Rae. "You haven't been into my room have you?"

"Or mine?" snapped Keller. "I don't want you in there."

"Me neither," snarled Cordell. "I'd better not catch you in there."

"Calm down, Mr. Cordell, Mr. Keller," Rae said firmly.

"That's right," said Cody. "Both of you, take it easy. We all agreed to help out Aunt Edith by cleaning rooms. The less we have to clean, the better. Especially if you don't appreciate it."

"Oh yeah? Well, I don't," Cordell replied. "Stay outta my room."

"Mine, too," said Keller. They stalked away.

"Well, my heavens, what a couple of rude fellows," said Ms. Wallace.

"I'll say," said Barber.

"Ought to teach *them* a lesson in manners, along with that young movie star," said McNab. He stepped out of his room and locked the door. "I think I'll go down to the garden and smell the flowers for a while." He walked toward the stairs.

"Whew! What a bunch," said Rae. "I guess that means I'm finished for the day—I've done my rooms."

"Why don't we show you that secret passage we told you about last night?"

"Fine, but I want to show you something first." Rae pulled a newspaper clipping from her pocket. "It's an article about a criminal. Check out the face in the photo."

The twins examined the clipping. It was Albert McNab!

"It says that he's a former doctor who became a con man."

Cody thought for a moment. "Looks like Ms. Wallace and Mr. Barber suspected it. But if that's Mr. McNab, why hasn't anyone done anything about it?"

"I wonder," said Otis.

Just then the door to Keller's room opened. "Gonna make this a double whammy," he muttered to himself. He locked his door and went downstairs.

"I think he's up to something right now," said Otis. "Let's follow him and see if we can find out what it is."

They followed Keller to the garden, where he approached McNab. They watched as the two got into a heated argument, shouting and waving their arms around. The twins and Rae couldn't hear what the men were saying, though.

After a while, things began to change. The voices got quieter—and then the angry faces began to smile. The scene ended with both of the men laughing. Keller ended up by slapping McNab on the back before he left the garden. When he was gone, McNab sat on a bench sunning himself, his eyes closed and his face turned to the sky. His mouth was curved in a quiet smile.

That was when Rae and the twins saw the wiry Winston Cato step out from behind a shrub and walk up the garden path. They were sure he had heard what had gone on.

"Mr. Cato, wait," Cody cried as he drew near them. "We want to ask you something."

"Still trying to figure things out?" Cato grinned.

"I guess you've got *us* figured out," Otis said. "Did you hear what Mr. Keller and Mr. McNab were talking about?"

"Yes, and it wasn't good—but it ended up all right. That Sam Keller is a sleazy guy. He tried to blackmail Mr. McNab. Claimed he found out he was really Horace Perkins, some criminal the law is looking for."

"But it seemed like they ended up as friends."

Cato chuckled. "That's right. Mr. McNab kept talking about his grocery business, and how he started thinking about going into it when he was a student at Kenmore High School in Arlington, Virginia. Turns out that's where Mr. Keller went to school—and they were in the same English class. Well, the two of them found out they had more in common—like they are both religious and belong to the same political party."

"*Sam Keller* is a religious man?" Cody asked in disbelief.

"I didn't think he was smart enough to pick a political party," said Otis.

Cato laughed. "I know, but there's more. It seems that both like to go to Las Vegas casinos. Well, pretty soon Mr. McNab has Mr. Keller convinced that he's a dead ringer for Mr. Perkins, but he's not Perkins."

Cato paused a moment and smiled broadly. "I believe him, too. That Mr. McNab is a nice guy. He's always pleasant. He didn't even hold it against Mr. Keller that he tried to blackmail him. Isn't that unbelievable?"

"Unbelievable, all right," said Rae.

"See you all later," said Cato, hurrying away.

"Well, we have more proof that Keller is a sleaze, but I don't know where we go with it," said Cody.

"So why don't we go down to the secret passage," said Otis.

Rae grinned. "Let's go."

✱

The boys nodded to each other. Then Otis pushed the button on the panel, the wall slid back, and they walked into the secret passage. Both carried their penlights, the narrow beams shining in the darkness. Rae switched on her own flashlight and followed.

The three of them felt their way down the steps and then headed into the winding tunnel. "It looks absolutely ancient," Rae breathed.

"Wait until you see what's up ahead," said Otis. "It's outrageous."

Before long, they were able to shut off the penlights. They could see that the rooms ahead were all lit up. They listened for voices as they walked.

Soon they were walking through the modern, freshly painted hallway, past the electronic equipment and the stacks and stacks of pirated DVDs. Just outside the lounge, they stopped to listen for voices.

Hearts pounding, they stood as still as statues. There was no sound coming from the lounge. They moved on, past more rooms stockpiled with equipment and DVDs, until they came to a smaller one near the end of the hall that was almost empty, except for a figure in a chair.

The three of them gasped when they recognized who it was. It was Steve Cordell!

[Chapter Fifteen]

Steve Cordell was tied to the chair. There was a gag in his mouth. Cody, Otis, and Rae hurried to untie him. He didn't thank them for it.

"How did you kids get down here?" he roared, spitting out pieces of the cotton gag.

"Why don't you start by thanking us for freeing you?" asked Cody.

"Then tell us who tied you up and why," said Otis.

"You can add a part about where all these bootleg DVDs and this equipment came from," said Rae.

Cordell stood up slowly and stretched. "I don't have any idea where this stuff came from," he said. Then he sneered. "It looks like your aunt Edith is running a little business on the side."

"Why you—" Cody began, taking a step toward him.

Otis put a hand on his arm. "Take it easy." He

turned to Cordell. "So is there an entrance to the secret passage in your room?"

Cordell rubbed his wrists where the ropes had bound him. It looked like he was stalling for time.

"Yeah, I found the panel in my room by accident."

"You didn't come down here and tie yourself up," Rae observed.

"Hey, I don't have to tell you anything," he said.

"We could call the police," Cody told him.

"Don't you dare," he began, but then changed his tune. "Oh, go ahead and call them. I don't care." He gave them a half-smile. "Look, I showed Keller the passage. He came down here with me. When I sat down, he put a sleeper hold on me. Then when I was out cold, he tied me up. It was just a prank."

"You call that a prank? You've got to be kidding," Cody blurted.

"Well, I'm not kidding," Cordell said. "Now, if you don't mind, I'm getting out of here."

"You aren't planning on leaving the inn, are you?" asked Otis.

"What I'm planning is my own business," Cordell replied. "But I'll tell you anyway. No, I'm not going anywhere." He walked out of the room.

$$\ast$$

"Prank? Getting bound and gagged is someone's idea of a joke?" After hearing the story, Aunt Edith was appalled. "I don't really want to see all that stuff in the secret passage, but I definitely have to call the police."

She let out a long sigh. "They'll send that awful Officer Tano again."

"Tell them to send somebody else, Aunt Edith," Cody insisted.

"Ask to speak to the police captain," Otis told her. "Tell him what happened the last time Tano came. He'll be interested to find out an officer treats a crime like a joke."

"I think we'll be able to prove that Officer Tano is involved in a cover-up," Cody added. "We think Mr. Cordell has been paying him off."

Aunt Edith gasped. Just then Ronnie Walker and Sam Keller walked by. They were carrying luggage, and both of them were grinning.

"Where are *they* going?" Otis asked.

Aunt Edith put a hand to her cheek. "They checked out earlier," she said. "Jamal is gone, too. Oh, dear, everyone is leaving . . . and now this business with the DVDs!"

"Where did *he* go?" Rae asked with a toss of her head. "Jamal, I mean."

"I don't know, dear. Ronnie Walker checked out for him."

"We should find out where Mr. Keller and Mr. Walker are headed," Cody said. He was already starting for the door. The others followed.

They found the two men loading luggage into separate cars. Otis ran to Ronnie Walker.

"Where's Jamal?"

Walker threw a bag into the car. "Jamal went over to Tacayno. He said he didn't like it here—it was too quiet and he couldn't get away from fans pestering him." Walker gave Rae and the twins a look that plainly said, "This means you."

"So you're going to join him there, and Keller is going with you?" Cody asked.

"I'm not going with him," squawked Keller. "We just happen to be leaving at the same time."

Keller turned around. He was sporting a shiner on his left eye. He rubbed at a smudge on his shirt. He opened his mouth to say something else but suddenly began jumping up and down and shouting, "Ow! Ow! Ow! Ow!"

He looked so comical that Rae and the twins couldn't help laughing. Ronnie Walker stared. "What's wrong with you, man? You goin' crazy?" he asked.

Keller ripped off his shirt. A large bumblebee flew out of it. "That thing stung me!" he fumed. There was a pink welt just below the tattoo on his shoulder. It was a picture of a gecko, with its mouth open as if it were laughing.

Keller flapped the shirt in the air a few times before putting it on again. "Bugs!" he snapped.

"A bee isn't a bug. It's an insect," Otis said.

"What? Get lost!" Keller waved a hand at Cody as he got into his car. Just then Steve Cordell rushed to the car and jumped in. He had a bag with him.

Keller's eyes widened and he shrank into the driver's seat. Cordell leaned toward him. "Don't worry, just drive. I'm with you now," he said.

After a moment, Keller started the car and sped away. Ronnie Walker followed. There was nothing Rae and the twins could do but watch them go.

"I wonder where Keller got that car," Rae said after a moment. "Jamal arrived on a yacht, and a car was on it. There aren't any other boats big enough to carry a car. There is no place to rent a car on the island."

"That's right." Otis snapped his fingers. "Winston Cato picked us up in a gray sedan. Sam Keller was driving a blue four-door. It looked like a real clunker, too."

"Yeah, it was no *racecar*, that's for sure," Cody agreed, adding one of his favorite palindromes.

"It's got to be one he kept here." Cody shrugged. "It proves that he's been here before. It doesn't help us figure out where he went with Cordell, though."

Otis and Cody looked at each other with furrowed brows. "There is something . . ." Cody began.

"Missing," Otis finished.

"It's about the . . ." Cody rubbed his brow.

"Tattoo," Otis said.

They looked at each other and their faces lit up. "You know it, too," Otis said to Cody. "The tattoo that Ronnie Walker called crazy."

"Keller didn't have that tattoo in the picture we found in Cordell's room. The picture was taken six years ago," said Cody.

"So if Walker hadn't seen Keller in six years, he wouldn't know about the tattoo," said Otis.

"Because the day Walker checked in, Keller was wearing a shirt that covered it."

"I noticed something else," said Rae. "Keller rubbed a smudge on his shirt. It was the same colors that were on Jamal Mason's bracelet."

"Really? Could they rub off?" asked Otis.

"Definitely. You see, Jamal mentioned that his friend thought the bracelet was from 1300 BC or earlier. In the Egyptian dynastic period from 3000 to 1250 BC, they didn't have a way to 'fix' dyes. That meant the dye wasn't colorfast. It could rub off or fade in the light. It hadn't, because it was in a box all this time. But now it should be preserved in a museum. I started to tell him, but he didn't want to listen."

Otis and Cody looked at her, wide-eyed. "You're amazing, Rae."

"A walking computer," said Otis. "So that color could have rubbed off onto the shirt during a struggle."

Cody was nodding. "Walker and Keller knew each other, and they probably got together recently. Since Keller and Cordell were brothers, it's a good bet that they *all* knew each other."

"And it's strange that they all happened to leave at the same time—and that Jamal was conveniently gone," said Otis.

"And how did Jamal get off the island, anyway?" Rae mused.

Cody spotted a piece of paper on the ground, picked it up, and examined it. "Bingo," he said. "This must have fallen out of Keller's pocket." He examined it. "It's a ransom note!"

Otis and Rae looked at the note.

Put two million dollars in unmarked bills in a bag. Then

wait for our call. We'll give you instructions on what to do next. If you

"It looks like they didn't finish it, but I've got a good idea who the note is about," said Otis.

Cody nodded. "Jamal."

"Where do you think they took him?" Rae asked, wringing her hands.

"Probably to their boat. It's got to be docked in the cove with the others," said Otis. "We have to hurry before they take off."

"But they have cars. We can't walk there fast enough," Cody said.

Cody and his brother looked at each other. They both said the words at the same time.

"The secret passage!"

A smile slowly spread across Otis's face. "We can even beat them there. They won't get away with this. I dare them to try."

Cody nodded. "*Go deliver a dare, vile dog!*" he said.

Otis looked at him and wrinkled his forehead. "So, who's a vile dog? Me?"

"Oh, no, no. . . . I didn't mean it that way," Cody said hurriedly. "I was only . . ."

"I know, I know," Otis sighed. "You had to come up with a palindrome."

[Chapter Sixteen]

"I'm glad you didn't say that we had to call the police first," Otis said to Cody.

"No way," his brother replied. "We don't have time. Aunt Edith will call them anyway. She was pretty upset about the pirated DVDs."

"I hope Jamal is all right," said Rae. Then she added, "Even though he *was* obnoxious."

The three were making their way along the passage that led from the bootleg processing center to the sea. Cody and Otis thought that it must lead to the cove where the boats were docked. They figured the pirates had docked there, too, and built the passage for a fast getaway.

It was obvious that the modern-day pirates had been using the passage, too. It was as clean and modern as the processing center. The walls had been drywalled and painted, and the floors had been tiled.

"Look, it forks up ahead," said Cody.

"Probably a trick to throw pursuers off the track," said Otis. "We've got to make sure that we're heading toward the cove. This way." He took the fork to the right.

A little while later they had to make another decision, and then another. There were many forks along the tunnel. There was the danger of traveling in circles. They brought along bread crumbs from the kitchen to mark their way so they wouldn't get lost. "Just like Hansel and Gretel," Cody had joked when they began.

It had been Rae's idea. She told them she'd read stories where secret passages had forks and turns set up to fool unwanted visitors.

When the tunnel went on and on, they all began to worry. What if they were on the wrong track? What if the crooks had already left with Jamal?

The tunnel curved to the left and ended in three forks. "Great," said Cody. "Well, Rae, it's just like in those stories after all."

"Three strikes and we're out," said Otis. "Let's make this a home run instead."

"Center fork," Cody said.

"Agreed," the twins heard from Rae.

"Agreed," Otis echoed.

They headed down the center fork. The passage grew narrower and narrower.

Then it came to a dead end.

"How could we have gone wrong?" Cody wailed.

Otis was examining the wall. "Maybe we didn't." He found a skeleton button in the bottom left-hand corner and pressed it. A panel slid open. Sunlight poured into the passage.

Cody grinned. "After you," he said, nodding to Rae.

Soon the three of them were standing in the sunshine. Now they had to find the right boat.

"Over there." Cody pointed. "It's got to be the boat with a laughing gecko on the side."

"Definitely," said Otis. "I don't see anyone on deck."

"They're around here somewhere," said Cody. "We've got to be careful." He looked from side to side and began to creep toward the gleaming white cabin cruiser with the green lizard on its side. The others followed.

The sea was still and not a single breeze stirred the air. The few other boats anchored near the *Laughing Gecko* looked empty.

The three rescuers boarded the boat cautiously. Otis pressed a finger to his lips and pointed belowdecks.

They all climbed down the ladder, trying to slow their pounding hearts. They were all repeating the same words to themselves: *focus . . . breathe.*

They found Jamal tied up on the floor in a corner of the galley. His eyes widened in surprise when he saw them. Once more, Otis cautioned against making any sound with a finger to his lips.

They had freed Jamal from all but his wrist bindings, when they heard footsteps on deck. Then suddenly two men came running toward them. It was Sam Keller and Steve Cordell.

"I knew you kids would be trouble," snarled Keller as he ran. His eyes bugged out and his face was red with fury. A vision of the man wearing a brown wig, mustache, and beard flashed before Cody's eyes as Keller lunged at him.

Each man grabbed a boy by the shoulders and held him in a viselike grip. Automatically, Cody and Otis raised their arms straight up in the break-out move their sensei had taught them. Both men were surprised to find their holds suddenly broken, their hands dangling in empty air as the boys streaked away with Rae running beside them.

"We'd better get help. I think we've got our proof now!" Otis blurted as he ran. Then Cordell jumped in front of him, blocking his path to the door. Otis cut to the right and ran to the corner of the boat where Jamal was tied.

Meanwhile, Keller caught Cody from behind. Cody gritted his teeth and stomped the man's instep with a heel kick. Keller gave a howl of pain and staggered backward. He regained his balance in an instant, lunged at Cody, and spun him around.

"So you wise guys have taken a couple of karate classes," he huffed. "Well, it's time to stop playing games."

Cody jerked himself free of Keller's grip. But then one of Keller's hands shot toward Cody's throat. Cody blocked his arm, grabbed his wrist, and twisted, whirling so that his back was to the man. He swept a foot back, hooked Keller's leg, and pulled it forward in a leg sweep.

This time Keller went down with a thud. His head hit the floor and he saw stars. *Boom!* He was out like a light.

Otis and Rae had been running circles around Cordell. He couldn't catch them, and it was making him madder and madder. He watched his brother fall down and fury exploded behind his eyes.

He ran toward Otis, shrieking, "I'm not going to let you ruin everything!" But he didn't get very far.

As he ran past Rae, she stuck out her foot and tripped him. *Thud!* Cordell hit the floor and joined his brother in la-la land.

Cody went over and felt each man's neck for a pulse. "These guys are okay . . . they're just out of it. We'd better tie them up before they come to."

The three boys quickly bound the men's hands and feet. Jamal looked down at them. "Scum," he muttered. Then he turned to the twins and their cousin. "Thanks for rescuing me. Do any of you know where my bodyguard is?"

Before either one of them could answer, Ronnie Walker appeared in the doorway. When he took in the scene, he turned to run away.

Jamal's mouth dropped open. "You were in on this," he whispered to himself. Then he called out sharply, "Stop right there, Ronnie! You can't run away. I'll have people find you wherever you go."

The sound of Walker's footsteps stopped suddenly. He trudged back slowly, appearing in the doorway with shoulders sagging.

Jamal was seething. "You were more than my bodyguard. I thought you were my friend. And this is how you repaid me."

[Chapter Seventeen]

No one trusted Ronnie Walker to drive, so the twins made him surrender his car keys. They made their way to his green sedan.

"Let's flip to see who drives," said Otis. He won the toss. "It's been a while but I'll be okay," he assured Jamal as he climbed behind the wheel.

Mr. Carson and Maxim had decided that the boys should learn to drive a few years ago. After all, they lived in the country and there just might be an emergency one day. They practiced on the back roads and were told again and again *never* to drive on their own except in a true emergency. This situation qualified.

When they reached the inn, Aunt Edith and the guests (except for Maxim, who was in the kitchen) were all sitting on the front porch, relaxing before dinner. Mr. Carson had returned from painting and was telling everyone about some beautiful birds he had seen. As the minutes ticked by everyone began wondering where Rae and the twins and the others were. They all stared in surprise as Jamal, Cody, Otis, and Rae arrived with Ronnie Walker slinking along behind. They gawked at the disheveled appearance of the group.

"What happened to you? What has been going on?" Mr. Carson cried.

Before anyone could answer, Maxim appeared, wiping his hands on his chef's apron. "Dinner is served!" he called brightly.

He gulped when he saw the new arrivals. "What . . . what have you people been *doing*? You all look like something the cat dragged in."

"Steve Cordell and Sam Keller tried to kidnap me, with the help of Ronnie here," said Jamal. "These three rescued me."

"They were holding him below deck on their boat," Cody added.

"Cordell and Keller were running the burner lab full of equipment and pirated DVDs," Otis told them. "We found more DVDs on the boat."

Nobody moved. They just sat and stared. It was plain to see that they were all having trouble processing the information.

"Isn't anyone going to phone the police?" Jamal asked, finally.

"I called earlier, when I heard about the DVDs in the secret passage," said Aunt Edith. "I specifically asked that they not send Officer Tano, but an operator said there was no one else available. He never showed up anyway."

The phone rang and she hurried to answer it. When she hung up, her face was pale. "That was the police chief," she said. "They found Officer Tano unconscious near the boating docks. Then they checked his call records and phoned. I told him what I just heard," she said. "He's coming right over."

Everyone turned to stare at Ronnie Walker. "Uh—Tano figured out that our DVD operation was blown and we'd be leaving the island," he said. "He came to the boat and wanted more money. He said he'd tell everyone we kidnapped Jamal. Cordell knocked him out. He wanted to do worse, but I talked him out of it."

"I hope you're telling the truth," said Maxim. "It would be the only decent thing you've done. Now we've just got to wait for the police chief."

"Wait a minute," said Otis. "We left Mr. Keller and Mr. Cordell tied up on the boat. They might escape."

Helen Wallace and Eric Barber stood up. "We'll go keep an eye on them."

"You two?" Maxim asked skeptically.

Helen Wallace laughed. "Oh, we're quite capable of guarding criminals. We've had lots of experience. Go on ahead. We'll explain later."

✳

Police Chief Dorado arrived at the inn moments later. It took almost an hour to tell him the whole story. Dorado listened patiently, asking questions from time to time. When he heard about the "accidents" that had been occurring at the inn and the way that Officer Tano had been treating them all as a joke, he was not amused.

"Officer Tano has been in on the operation for a long time," admitted Walker. "He was paid to look the other way."

The chief clasped his hands together. "I want to hear everything you know about this, Mr. Walker," he said. "The whole story. Don't leave out a single thing. Cooperation is the only way to make things easier for yourself."

Walker nodded and launched into his story. It grew more and more amazing.

"We . . . the three of us . . . work for Moe Kleese. He's been using the island as a hideout and a base of operations for his pirated DVD business, and other rackets as well, since the nineties. He never bought the inn because it had been abandoned for years. He thought that buying it would only draw attention to his activities. He never dreamed that anyone *else* would want to buy it."

He threw up his hands. "Then this woman buys the place from the government for cash. Before anybody knew what was going on, there was a problem."

Walker shifted in his seat. "'Steve Cordell' is an alias for Jimmy Black, also known as Bobo. The guy who's been calling himself 'Sam Keller' is his brother, John, also known as Jojo. Bobo and Jojo have been part of Moe's gang for a long time. We did some jobs together years ago, and they recruited me to help in their kidnapping plan."

"Was that when you were Jamal's bodyguard?" asked the chief.

Walker nodded. "I was going to stay out of crime, but they talked about so much money I couldn't refuse. They figured it was enough so they could stop working for Kleese, and there would be plenty for me, too. All I had to do was convince Jamal and his parents that he should come to Calavera Island. It was easy."

Walker took a sip of water. "When Kleese found

out that someone was opening an inn, he sent Jojo to pose as a worker. He made sure that things would go wrong. Later, when he came back to the island, Bobo helped out with it. They were trying to scare people away and shut down the inn, but it didn't work."

Walker went on to tell about the kidnapping plans. He blamed Bobo for messing things up.

"Cordell—Bobo—got nervous. He said someone was poking his nose into things here and kidnapping might bring the law on us. Keller—Jojo—wanted to go ahead with the plan. He got Bobo down in the secret passage and tied him up."

Walker gulped some more water. "When Bobo found out that these three"—he pointed to Rae and the twins—"had discovered the secret passage, he knew he couldn't save the operation. Best to join the kidnapping plan and get away from the Boss. He's gonna be real mad when he finds out his operation is blown," he said.

"It was that Jojo guy who grabbed me," said Jamal. "That lowlife snuck into my room with chloroform. I got a good look at him before I passed out, though."

Walker sighed. "It was supposed to be simple. We figured that Jamal would be asleep and he wouldn't even know who kidnapped him. We were going to smuggle him out of the inn onto the island of Tacayno.

We'd collect the ransom, split up, and make a phone call to the inn. By the time someone came to get him, we'd be long gone."

"But I'd have found you," said Jamal. "I've got enough money to get people searching everywhere in the world."

Walker rubbed his eyes. "I didn't mean you any harm," he said.

Jamal gave him a long look. "You didn't care," he said. "You were only thinking of the money."

He turned to look at Cody, Otis, and Rae. "I owe you guys an apology," he said. "I really acted like a jerk. I guess all the success went to my head. I thought I was all that, but I wasn't. It's about time I grew up."

✳

Later that evening, after the police had taken Steve Cordell and Sam Keller away, and everyone had finished Maxim's delicious dinner, Albert McNab said, "I think it's time that we cleared up another mystery." He looked at Helen Wallace and Eric Barber. "Don't you folks have a confession to make?"

Ms. Wallace and Mr. Barber looked at each other with twinkling eyes. "Shall you start, Eric, or shall I?"

Barber rolled his eyes. "I'll start, but jump in

anytime," he said. He took a deep breath. "Helen and I aren't a retired librarian and a shoe store owner."

"I knew it," Otis said, amazed. He looked at Cody. "I told you, right? They were hiding something."

Cody nodded. "That's right. You did."

"Well, you're a smart young man, Otis. Mr. Barber and I work together. We're private investigators," Ms. Wallace said.

"Huh?" Cody and Otis both said at once.

"Well, you had me fooled," said Maxim.

"Me, too," said Mr. Carson.

"Oh, wow, this is too much," said Jamal. "It's funny to think that two private investigators missed cracking the biggest case here."

Barber shook his head. "Imagine, it was right under our noses and you boys solved it."

"You certainly did," Ms. Wallace agreed. "However, Eric and I were focused on another case."

"Which turned out to be totally groundless," said Barber with a sigh.

McNab chuckled. "They were chasing *me*."

"You?" Otis said in surprise.

"That's right," said Ms. Wallace.

"We got an anonymous tip that the famous doctor-turned-forger was here on the island. We figured it was

McNab, but every time we talked to him we had our doubts," Barber explained.

"He had childhood pictures in front of his father's grocery store and letters from his scouting troop," said Ms. Wallace.

"And his eyes were the wrong color. Horace Perkins has blue eyes. McNab's are brown."

"Then we got another anonymous call here at the inn, from a woman," said Ms. Wallace. "She said that the first call had been made by Perkins himself to throw us off the track. He was actually back in Irons, Michigan."

"So that's why your room was ransacked, Mr. McNab," Rae said.

"That's right." McNab chuckled, crinkling his nose. "I was so angry, and I couldn't understand it because nothing was taken."

Still chuckling, McNab slapped his knee. "Now, I liked these two at first," he said, thumbing in the direction of the investigators. "But as time went on, they started to drive me crazy. They were always following me around everywhere I went, asking me the dumbest questions. I thought they were nuts."

Helen Wallace laughed. "I don't wonder."

"It made no sense to me," said McNab. "I kept

saying I sold groceries. I really thought they were crazy. Now I know what they were up to. Well, time for me to turn in. It'll be the first good night's sleep I've had in a while. I kept thinking I'd see one of 'em pop out of a dresser drawer while I was nodding off."

"Wait a minute, Mr. McNab," said Aunt Edith. "I want everyone to take a look at my nephew's latest painting." She went over to an easel covered with a drapery. She pulled the cloth away to reveal a beautiful picture of the inn at sunset. Just barely visible was a pirate peering around the corner of the building.

Everyone oohed and aahed. "It's great," said McNab. "But I hope we don't hear from that pirate's ghost tonight. I need some rest."

One by one, the other guests said good night. Soon there were only Rae and the twins, along with Maxim, Mr. Carson, and Aunt Edith.

"Too bad we never found that buried treasure," Cody said. He yawned and stood up. "See you in the morning."

"Just a moment," said Mr. Carson. "I want to show you where I got the idea to do a painting of the inn at sunset. It's from an old picture Aunt Edith showed me. It's hanging in the hall."

"I found it in a trunk in one of the rooms upstairs,"

said Aunt Edith. "It was wrapped in a cloth, framed and everything. I'm so glad it was in such good condition. The frame looks so old. Come on and I'll show you."

They all walked into the hallway to have a look at the painting. "It's old, all right," said Cody.

Otis gasped. "Look at that!" He pointed to a tiny skull in the corner of the picture. He gently took the painting from the wall. The backing was loose and it pulled away when he took the picture down.

"Oh dear, do be careful with it," cried Aunt Edith.

"There's something under here," said Otis. He was right. Underneath the loose backing was a treasure map on yellowed parchment, with a red skull marking a particular spot near the inn.

"The pirate forgot where he put his own clue!" Cody marveled.

As soon as the words were out of his mouth a wind blew open the French doors at the end of the dining room. The curtains blew and the plates on the table rattled.

The map flew from Otis's hand and spiraled into the air. As they watched, spellbound, the page blew out through the open doors. And then the gust of wind died down as suddenly as it had sprung up.

Cody rubbed the goose bumps that had appeared on his arms. "Spooky," he said.

Otis and Rae shivered. "Yeah," Otis agreed. "But don't worry. I got a good look at that map. I know where the treasure is buried."

He led them to a corner of a stone wall behind the inn. Then he and Cody got shovels from the garden shed and began to dig. Soon the shovels struck something hard. Not long afterward, they pulled a trunk from the ground.

It took a long time, but they finally busted open the lock with a hammer. They were amazed at what they found inside.

"It's buried treasure, all right," Cody said with satisfaction. He held up a golden goblet. There were others inside, along with jewelry and gold doubloons.

Mr. Carson lifted up a goblet and borrowed Cody's penlight. He shone light on the underside of the base. "Mendoza," he whispered. "This is part of the lost treasure of Count Francisco Mendoza. It was stolen from one of his ships by pirates."

"By Black Heart's crew," said Cody. "The pirate ghost can stop looking for it now."

[Chapter Eighteen]

One week after the trip to Calavera Island, the Carsons, Maxim, and Rae were gathered in the den of the Carson house. Maxim rattled his newspaper.

"Listen to this, everybody," he said with excitement. "They caught the con man! Barber and Wallace did it. They found him in Paris. It was McNab after all. And guess who was with him? Muriel Esposito! She was calling herself Sally Perkins, though. She was his wife!"

"Wow, he gave quite a performance, right up to the end," said Otis.

"That's right." Cody gave him a little shove. "So much for your book about spotting liars. Mr. McNab and Ms. Esposito were the only ones you trusted."

Otis scowled at him. "Well, there were plenty of other liars there who gave themselves away from the beginning. But I have to admit that Mr. McNab was an *expert* liar," he said. "He must have enjoyed having a joke on all of us."

"Right," Rae agreed. "But he made a mistake when he left his brown contact lenses in the lobby to be found after he left. He meant to tweak everyone's noses, but it started the investigators on his trail again."

"He wore colored contact lenses. He had doctored photographs. Imagine, we all fell for it! Dumb." Cody punched the air.

"I should have known when Winston Cato told us about that conversation he overheard between Mr. McNab and Sam Keller. Mr. McNab conned him the same way he conned Ms. Wallace and Mr. Barber and everybody else."

"Why should you have known?" asked Rae.

"I once read an article about a man named Victor Lustig, a con man from back in the 1920s. He was famous for conning somebody into buying the Eiffel Tower. Lustig roped in his victims by pretending to be just like them . . . same politics, same religion. And he was always interested in them, never bored."

Otis shook his head. "I was really stupid not to figure him out." He snorted. "He even sat there talking to us all about convincing Mr. Barber and Ms. Wallace they were wrong about him." Otis mimed a thumb and forefinger in the shape of an "L" on his forehead.

Mr. Carson looked up from his sketch pad and saw it. "Oh, stop that," he said. "I think it's *awesome*, as you would say, that you all caught those crooks. And you found treasure that has been placed in a museum in Spain. I'm proud of you."

"Thanks, Dad," Otis said. He thought for a moment. "Y'know, Aunt Edith ought to change the travel agents she uses. They didn't send people who wanted to get away from it all. They sent people who were *running* away from it all."

"You mean running from *the law*," quipped Cody. Everyone chuckled.

Maxim peered over his newspaper and smiled. "They've finally got the biggest crook of all—Moe Kleese—scrambling. He's having a hard time trying to prove he had nothing to do with the pirated DVD scam. He tried to hang the whole thing on the two brothers, but they sang like a couple of canaries."

"Well, Moe Kleese is a pretty slick guy," Mr. Carson mumbled, his eyes on his sketchbook. "I'm happy that Aunt Edith won't have any more trouble with his gang. Maybe now she can enjoy some success with her inn."

"Well, it got her some publicity, that's for sure,"

said Rae. "The inn has been mentioned every day in the paper, and it's all over TV and the Internet."

"Jamal will make sure she keeps getting media attention when the buzz over the DVD case dies down," said Cody. "He said he'd have his own publicity people make sure she gets coverage from time to time. Plus, he promised to spread the word about the inn himself."

"Hey, there's Jamal now!" Otis pointed to the TV screen. "Look."

Jamal was talking to a reporter. A banner that read *Jamal Mason talks about his stay at Caribbean inn* crawled across the bottom of the screen. Cody turned up the sound and everyone listened eagerly.

"I want to tell everyone what a wonderful place the Calavera Inn is. The island scenery is so beautiful, I can't say so enough. The snorkeling is right up there with some of the best I've experienced in places like Cozumel. There are so many beautiful animals. I think there are almost five hundred kinds of birds on that little island, so you see them a lot."

Jamal looked into the camera and smiled. "Is the inn haunted by a pirate? I don't know. I know it certainly seemed like there was a ghost around, but he didn't try to hurt anybody. I'd say, see for yourself.

Who knows? Now that the treasure has been found, he might not be back. On the other hand, he might decide to stick around."

He stopped smiling and turned serious. "I have to say that I don't know what would have happened to me if it hadn't been for my good friends Cody and Otis Carson and Rae Lee. Life isn't like the movies, and I didn't have any special powers to help me when those kidnappers were holding me prisoner," he said. "If you guys are watching, I want to thank you once more for coming to my rescue."

"Wow!" the twins shouted.

Rae grinned. "That was so awesome!"

Jamal smiled again. "I hope you guys are hearing this. We are definitely on for a visit. I'll call you in about a week. Bye for now!" Jamal waved to the camera, and his face faded from the screen.

"Jamal turned out to be really cool in the end," said Cody.

"The coolest," Otis added. "He's doing lots of stuff to help Aunt Edith. He helped her find a new cook and another guide and a maid."

"He's quite a guy," said Mr. Carson.

"Quite a guy. Quite a guy," echoed Pauly the parrot. "Give him a treat!"

Dude was lying on the carpet next to Cody. When he heard the word "treat," he jumped up and wagged his tail. *Woof!* he barked eagerly and began to trot toward the kitchen.

"Uh-oh," Cody whispered. "I think Pauly is setting the dog up."

Sure enough, the next words that erupted from the parrot's beak were, "Sit down! Roll over!"

Just like always, Dude fell for it. He snapped into a sitting position, and then whirled into a roll. When he heard the parrot cackle, he growled and slunk into another room.

Everyone laughed. Then Otis scowled at the bird. "Shame on you, Pauly. It's a good thing Dude isn't a *bird dog.*"

Cody thought for a moment. He was trying to come up with a palindrome to follow Otis's pun. "No, Dude isn't a *bird dog,*" he said finally. "And he's smarter than he seems. He's a *dog god.*"

Maxim groaned at the corny palindrome. Everyone else laughed.